Look what people are saying about Stephanie Bond...

4 stars! "Sex and humor blend perfectly...this fairy tale of a story has the perfect magic ending."
—*Romantic Times BOOKreviews* on *No Peeking...*

"Blazing hot...will have you planning your own fantasy."
—*CataRomance* on *In a Bind*

"A burning-hot hero, and the sex explodes."
—*Romantic Times BOOKreviews* on *Watch and Learn*

"*My Favorite Mistake* certainly illustrates the author's gift for weaving original, brilliant romance that readers find impossible to put down."
—*Wordweaving.com*

"*This* is a sexy book."
—*Romance Reading Room* on *My Favorite Mistake*

"Sassy, ultra-sexy."
—*Romantic Times BOOKreviews* on *Cover Me*

"A tremendous tale of hidden desires and dreams that is delightfully risqué and full of charm."
—*Romance Junkies* on *She Did a Bad, Bad Thing*

Blaze

Dear Reader,

I'd like to introduce you to the members of the Red Tote Book Club—a group of women who meet regularly to discuss the greatest erotic literature ever written. But things really get interesting when they decide to put words into action and use the lessons inside the books they read to seduce the men of their dreams!

Follow Cassie as she shows a former boyfriend who was "just not into her" exactly what he missed! And shy, administrative assistant Page, who undergoes a role reversal of the most exciting kind to seduce her boss. And party girl Wendy, who's determined to convince her lifelong best friend that they can be friends *with benefits*. And finally, Jacqueline, with her "take no prisoners" business reputation, who concedes her desire to *submit* to an intriguing new client.

I hope you enjoy this special collection of connected novellas written especially to celebrate the release of the 500th book in the Harlequin Blaze series! Please let your friends know about the wonderful love stories you find between the pages of Harlequin novels. Visit me at www.stephaniebond.com.

Happy reading,

Stephanie Bond

Stephanie Bond

SEDUCTION BY THE BOOK

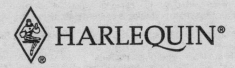

HARLEQUIN®

TORONTO • NEW YORK • LONDON
AMSTERDAM • PARIS • SYDNEY • HAMBURG
STOCKHOLM • ATHENS • TOKYO • MILAN • MADRID
PRAGUE • WARSAW • BUDAPEST • AUCKLAND

Recycling programs for this product may not exist in your area.

ISBN-13: 978-0-373-79504-8

SEDUCTION BY THE BOOK

ABOUT THE AUTHOR

Stephanie Bond believes in the power of books to change a person's life. Reading and writing have taken her on wonderful journeys, real and imagined, and brought her friendships of a lifetime. Stephanie lives in midtown Atlanta and has, in her words, "the best job in the world."

Books by Stephanie Bond

HARLEQUIN BLAZE
2—TWO SEXY!
169—MY FAVORITE MISTAKE
282—JUST DARE ME…
338—SHE DID A BAD, BAD THING
428—WATCH AND LEARN
434—IN A BIND
440—NO PEEKING…

MIRA BOOKS
BODY MOVERS
BODY MOVERS: 2 BODIES FOR THE PRICE OF 1
BODY MOVERS: 3 MEN AND A BODY
4 BODIES AND A FUNERAL
5 BODIES TO DIE FOR
6 KILLER BODIES

For Brenda.
A thousand thanks.

Prologue

GABRIELLE POPE STARED AT the clock on the wall, willing the minute hand to tick just one more time. A bead of perspiration rolled between her shoulder blades. After ignoring her silent pleas all day to move faster, the clock was finally straining toward six o'clock. She leaned forward in her chair as the second hand swept around slowly…slowly…

The minute hand sprang to twelve without incident, but Gabrielle's pulse skipped as wildly as if an alarm had sounded.

Time for book club.

She pushed back from her tiny desk at one of the oldest branches of the Atlanta Public Library and stood. As she guided the stiff chair under her desk, the warm flush climbing her neck belied her careful movements. Gabrielle leaned over to pick up her red book tote—the special tote that held the special books. Then, guarding a secret smile, she nodded to coworkers and patrons as she made her way through the maze of hallways.

The sprawling building had undergone several renovations and additions over the years, rendering some areas less desirable. Tucked behind an abandoned supply closet was a forgotten room that held six of the most plush, most comfortable chairs Gabrielle could find, situated around an elegant table with curving legs.

The room was rarely used. Employees and patrons complained the low lighting was unsuitable for reading, the dark corners and flaking plaster walls, depressing. But the Red Tote Book Club found the space atmospheric, and perfect for sipping tea or smuggled-in wine during their monthly get-togethers.

Gabrielle moved around the room, dusting lightly and straightening the chairs. At the sound of a rap on the door, she looked up and smiled as four members filed in, talking and laughing amongst themselves. They greeted Gabrielle, each turning a smile in her direction as they claimed a chair. The women were all in their early to mid-thirties, and from their appearances, each of them had come directly from their jobs.

Cassie Goodwin was an architect with shoulder-length hair the color of strong coffee, and intelligent blue eyes. Her smart chinos and long-sleeve button-up shirt were neat and modest, while her practical shoes were dusty, presumably from a job site. Cassie was friendly to everyone, but there was a wariness about her that hinted of past heartache.

Page Sharpe, a shy administrative assistant, might as well have been dressed in camouflage. She pushed a fat plait of auburn-colored hair over the shoulder of a drab dress that said, "Don't look at me." Her expression and emerald green eyes were demure, but Gabrielle had seen for herself the way Page lit up during their book discussions. She was a banked fire, that one.

Wendy Trainer, by comparison, was a pixie blonde firecracker who was always ready with a joke and a laugh. She'd found her niche as a party planner. Her exuberant, funky clothing reflected a gregarious personality, but Gabrielle suspected that Wendy used humor to cover for loneliness.

Jacqueline Mays was undoubtedly the most reserved woman Gabrielle had ever met. The auditor's black hair was wound into a tight bun, her pale skin flawless, her hazel eyes, unflinching. Her slender body was bound up in a mannish suit. Gabrielle wondered if the woman even needed the severe black glasses she wore, or if Jacqueline used them as a shield.

Everyone had their secret reasons for being here.

As they each revealed goodies they'd brought to share—chocolates, fresh strawberries, cheesecake bites, and wine, both red and white to suit each person's taste, the door opened and their last member strode in.

As always, Gabrielle noted, Carol Snow managed to separate herself from the group. She arrived alone and left alone. Of all the women, Carol had also revealed the least about herself. After meeting for over six months, Gabrielle couldn't get a fix on the beauty whose hair was the color of brass and whose clothes were of the highest quality. But from Carol's comments on the books they read, Gabrielle had gathered that the woman had a motive for everything she did. As was customary, Carol nodded hello to everyone and locked the door to dissuade accidental snooping.

As the women settled in, Gabrielle glanced around the room. So different, all of them. Yet something had compelled each one of them to respond to her online ad about a new kind of book club for women who were looking to add a little spice to their entertainment reading. Some part of her had feared and expected the respondents to be women with blatantly subversive interests. But to her delight, all five women were not only strangers to each other, but discreet and largely unassuming. Yet they didn't shrink when, at that first meeting, Gabrielle had passed around a suggested reading list of the best erotic literature ever written.

It was party-girl Wendy who had suggested that they each buy a red tote of their choice to stow their steamy books, and the Red Tote Book Club was born. To outsiders, their group had the appearance of just another stuffy book club. Only the members were privy to the decadent recitations as they each read aloud their favorite scenes, and to the candid conversations afterward as they discussed shifting sexual roles throughout history and in contemporary times.

As Gabrielle glanced over the members, affection filled her heart. She was older than the other women, approaching forty. And she was alone. In fact, the one thing the six women had in common was that none of them were in a committed relationship. But she didn't want the younger women to make the same mistakes she had, to wait until it was too late to find a loving partner. Part of the allure of being around books all the time was her affinity for happy endings. And she'd decided it was time for a field trip, so to speak.

After the wine was poured and the delicacies passed around, Gabrielle addressed the group. "This evening, I have a challenge for you. I asked you to be thinking about the one book we've read over the past few months that resonated with you, and why. Have you made your selections?"

The women shrugged and nodded in turn.

"Good," Gabrielle said. "Because I'd like for you to take the book club material one step further."

She paused and looked around at the expressions of anticipation—some eager, some anxious.

Gabrielle wet her lips. "I dare you to take the book that most spoke to you, that most *changed* you. Then each of you pick a month and, using that book's themes and lessons…seduce the man of your dreams. Putting the words into action, so to speak."

The room vibrated with shocked silence. Eyes widened and smiles faltered. Glances were exchanged. The women shifted in their chairs.

"Seducing a man is a strange assignment for a book club," Carol Snow remarked, her voice suspicious. "Why would you ask us to do something like that?" Carol's body language was suddenly nervous. She glanced around the corners of the ceiling, as if she were afraid they were on hidden camera.

Of the five members, Gabrielle realized, Carol was the most skittish about sex and love. She would be the hardest one to win over. Gabrielle hesitated, then inclined her head. "A fair question. And the truth is, I don't want you to be alone when you're pushing forty, like me, and asking yourself 'what if?'"

She spread a smile over the group. "In each of you, I detect a timidity about your own sexuality, yet you were brave enough to join this book club. That tells me that whatever part of yourself you've repressed, you have a secret desire to let it out. That's what this assignment is all about. Letting it out. Being your authentic sexual self. Still, it's up to each of you to decide if seducing the man of your dreams is...worthwhile."

Gabrielle's heart thudded, half expecting the women to bolt for the door, with Carol Snow in the lead. If so, her grand experiment would be over before it had begun. If these younger women were successful in seducing the men of their dreams with the confidence gained from reading the book club books, she planned to try it herself. But if this group of young, vibrant women failed, she was doomed.

The air was heavy with anticipation. Then, one by one, they met her gaze.

"Okay," Cassie said, angling her chin. "I'm in."

"What do I have to lose?" Page said with a shrug.

"I'm up for it," Wendy offered.

"I'm willing to give it a try," Jacqueline agreed.

All eyes turned to Carol, who seemed to be struggling with the concept.

"The assignment is optional, of course," Gabrielle interjected. "No one should feel pressured to do something they don't want to do."

Carol pursed her mouth, then murmured, "I'll think about it."

"Excellent," Gabrielle said, clasping her hands. "This will be fun, you'll see. And life-changing. You're each going to need a target and a plan."

"And more wine," Wendy quipped. She raised her glass. "Here's to seduction by the book!"

They all clinked their plastic glasses together, although Carol was slow in joining.

As the bittersweet sting of the red wine flowed over

her throat, Gabrielle happily surveyed the flushed, animated faces and wondered how each woman would rise to the erotic challenge. Let the experiment begin.

BETWEEN THE COVERS

1

CASSIE GOODWIN WONDERED if her face was as crimson
as it felt. From a plastic cup she took a deep drink of
cool white wine that had been smuggled into the library
for the monthly meeting of the Red Tote Book Club.
The sweet, sharp tang of the sauvignon blanc flowed
over her tongue as the shocking words of the group's
coordinator, Gabrielle Pope, still reverberated in Cassie's head.

*I dare you to take the book that most spoke to you,
that most changed you, and use the book's themes and
the lessons to seduce the man of your dreams.*

When Cassie had seen the ad posted on a local Web
site about a book club for women who wanted to add
a little spice to their entertainment reading, she'd been
intrigued...and a little scared, not knowing what she
might be walking into. But since the meeting was to
convene in a public place, she'd told herself she would
be safe. And that she could leave if she found the group
to be populated with abrasive, subversive types who
made her uncomfortable.

To her surprise, the four other women who had
joined the group that first night were normal...boring,
even—with the exception of Wendy Trainer, who had

bounded into the room like a popular girl on the first day of school. Her disarming smile and witty chatter lured the other members—Cassie, Page Sharpe, Jacqueline Mays and Carol Snow—out from behind their sunglasses and nervous expressions.

Cassie had always been a voracious reader, but had never considered herself the book club type. For her, reading was a private pleasure, enjoyed in bits of precious leisure time here and there. For the short time she and fellow architect Mark Shapiro had dated, she'd barely had time to read her mail, much less an entire book.

But after Mark had unceremoniously dumped her, she was suddenly left with a lot of free time. Sagging under a battered ego, she'd tucked in many a chilly night with a good book to keep her company. And in the process, she'd rediscovered her love of reading. The Red Tote Book Club had come along at the perfect time for Cassie. The camaraderie over discussing classic erotic novels made her feel connected again…and the naughty content between the covers made her feel feminine again.

But the dare from Gabrielle, for the members to put words into action, had caught her by surprise.

And Cassie was still reeling over the fact that she'd been the first person in the group to pipe up and accept the challenge.

Mark's face had popped into her mind immediately, along with his parting words…

Sorry, Cassie—I think you're a great girl, but…I guess we're just not that into each other. Something's missing…

Meaning, she didn't turn him on.

His brush-off had blindsided her, left her flat-footed and speechless. Partly because she'd attributed Mark's friendly hugs and chaste good-night kisses to the behavior of a classic southern gentleman. She'd been content to let things simmer while they got to know each other.

Meanwhile, Mark had apparently mistaken her lack of sexual initiative for disinterest.

And when he'd broken up with her, she hadn't known how to tell him that, in fact, she lay awake every night thinking about the two of them intertwined. She'd been more attracted to Mark than any man she'd ever dated, but she'd held back because Mark was such a catch and she hadn't wanted to mess things up by coming across as promiscuous or desperate. Besides, they were in the same industry. Even in a city the size of Atlanta their paths still crossed occasionally and they had mutual acquaintances in the field of architecture. She had a reputation to uphold.

On the other hand, she missed Mark—missed his tilting smile and his zest for life. She'd agonized over approaching him and suggesting they give their relationship another chance. After all, they enjoyed each other's company and had much in common. They'd shared great conversations over meals they prepared together and during long hikes. But when Mark had looked at her with desire, it had left her so tongue-tied, she could only look away or change the subject. In hindsight, she hadn't given him any reason to think they would light up the sheets.

So many times since their abrupt goodbye Cassie had wondered how she could change Mark's perception of her, and now, Gabrielle had just offered her the framework.

"Earth to Cassie."

Cassie blinked to find fellow book club member Wendy waving a hand in front of her face. "Sorry—did I miss something?"

Their leader, Gabrielle, gave her an indulgent smile. "I was saying that since you spoke up first, you must already have a man in mind."

"I do," Cassie murmured, glancing around at the other women. They gathered in a forgotten room of the library, in low lighting and comfortable chairs. In the center of the table were decadent foodstuffs they'd each contributed to share—fruit, chocolate, pastries.

"Does that mean you're willing to go first?" Gabrielle asked.

Cassie took a deep breath, then nodded. "Yes, I'll go first."

"Excellent. Can you tell us more about this man you want to seduce?" Gabrielle prodded gently.

Cassie hesitated. "I don't want to get into specifics, but he's someone I used to date. I was half in love with him and I always thought we deserved another chance."

"Why did you break up?" Page Sharpe, a shy auburn-haired woman spoke tentatively, as if she didn't expect Cassie to answer her.

Cassie shifted in her chair. "I might have given off some wrong signals. I believe he thought I wasn't interested in…sex."

"But you were?" Jacqueline Mays asked. The woman's pale, anxious expression, intimated that she knew a thing or two about repression.

"Oh, absolutely," Cassie, said, fanning her hot face.

The women all laughed, as if they were surprised she

had admitted it. Did she really present such a dull exterior to the world?

"What kept you from letting him know you were attracted to him?" Wendy asked. The furrow in her brow indicated that she might have more than just a passing interest in Cassie's answer.

Cassie took another drink of wine while she considered the question. "My older sister was promiscuous. I guess I erred in the other direction. I want sex to mean something. But with this guy, I guess I hesitated too long and missed my chance."

"It's never too long to wait if it's right for you," Gabrielle assured her. "What makes you think you're ready now?"

"Distance has given me perspective," she said. "And the books we've read and shared in this room have made me realize that wanting sex is natural and healthy."

"And fun," added Wendy, licking chocolate off her fingers.

All the women laughed.

"Is there a particular book we've read you think might help you approach this man about giving your relationship another chance?" Gabrielle asked.

Cassie nodded. "*Lady Chatterley's Lover* by D. H. Lawrence."

"A wonderful book," Gabrielle agreed, and the others chorused their approval. "But why *Lady Chatterley's Lover?*"

"I guess because Connie was proactive about changing her love life," Cassie offered.

"You mean, her *sex* life," Carol Snow, the loner of the group, said.

"Yes," Cassie agreed. "She saw Mellors, the groundskeeper, and she went after him. I suppose that's what I need to do."

"And do you have a plan for seducing your man?" Jacqueline asked.

Cassie bit her lip. "Not yet."

"Connie met Mellors while walking through the forest," Page ventured. "Is there a place where you can accidently-on-purpose run into your former boyfriend?"

A smile curved Cassie's mouth. She'd seen the firm that Mark worked for listed as a competitor bidding for a job her firm was also bidding on. "I can think of a few reasons for our paths to cross."

"That's a start," Gabrielle agreed, then addressed the group. "What kinds of things can Cassie borrow from Connie Chatterley's behavior to help guide her?"

"Connie made herself available to Mellors," Jacqueline said. "She went out of her way to let him know she was open to a physical relationship. She sought him out."

"Good. What else?"

"The fact that their relationship was secretive seemed to heighten the experience for both of them," Wendy offered.

Jacqueline nodded. "Men, especially, enjoy the adrenaline kick they get from doing something that seems forbidden."

"So take him by surprise," Page said.

"And be extra naughty," Jacqueline added.

A sense of excitement whipped through the room and Cassie realized that while the women were talking about her proposed seduction, they were already thinking ahead to their own plans. Only Carol Snow seemed to hold herself apart from the group's growing enthusiasm.

And Cassie wasn't without her own reservations. "But what if he…turns me down?"

"That's a risk you have to be willing to take," Gabrielle said.

"Yeah, what's the worst thing that can happen?" Wendy pressed.

"I'd be humiliated," Cassie said.

"But what's the *best* thing that could happen?" Page asked.

"Salvaging what could be a great relationship for both of us," Cassie said.

"So you have to be willing to put it all out there," Jacqueline added.

Gabrielle sat back and clasped her hands. "Lady Chatterley's decision to seduce Mellor turned into a wonderful, but problematic, love affair. Will you be okay if you're able to seduce this man, but a long-term relationship doesn't work out?"

Cassie's heart fluttered with teetering indecision for a few seconds, then resolve set in. "Yes. This is something I want to prove I can do, and this man is someone I'd feel safe with."

"Well, then…" Gabrielle smiled. "Good luck!"

"We'll be rooting you on from the sidelines," Wendy said. "Send us text updates to let us know what's going on."

"That's a good idea," Page chorused, and the group coordinated their text addresses.

"Are you excited to be first?" Jacqueline murmured.

Cassie nodded as anticipation flowered in her chest

like an orchid. She suddenly felt so alive and so…self-aware. Desire quivered through her midsection. Her breasts felt heavy. She lifted the glass of wine to press against her heated cheek and thought of all the delicious things she had planned for Mark. She reached for a plump strawberry and considered its ruby perfection before sinking her teeth into it. The sweet juices flooded her mouth and she nearly moaned with pleasure.

It was as if she were tasting a strawberry for the first time.

I guess we're just not that into each other. Something's missing…

Mark Shapiro, Cassie vowed, would live to eat his words.

2

MARK SHAPIRO HAD BOTH HANDS around a thick burger when his cell phone rang.

"Leave it, man," his coworker Steve Hamlin said with a wave. "Whatever it is, it can wait until after lunch."

Mark glanced at the caller ID as the phone flashed from the table. At the sight of the name CASSIE GOODWIN, his brow furrowed in surprise. Cassie had been on his mind ever since he'd seen her firm listed as a competitor bidding for the Belzer Tower job his firm was also bidding on. He realized that he missed her. But why would Cassie be calling after—how long had it been? Six months?

Steve glanced down. "Uh-oh. When an ex-girlfriend calls, it can't be good news. What if she's pregnant?"

Mark shot Steve a glare. "Trust me—if she's pregnant, the baby's not mine."

It wasn't that he hadn't wanted in Cassie's bed. She was a looker and smart as a whip, but she was just too...*tame* to get his blood going. After surviving a serious illness as a teen, Mark prided himself on having a passion for everything in life, and he wanted the same in his partner. At times he had detected chemistry between him and Cassie, but when he'd moved in for anything more than a kiss, he'd always gotten shut down. Still, he'd had his fantasies about her long legs and her full breasts—

"Wait a minute," Steve said, cutting into Mark's thoughts. "Doesn't Cassie work for Rugers and Associates?"

"Yeah."

"They're bidding on the Belzer Tower project, too." Steve gestured. "Answer it. Find out what you can about their bid."

Mark frowned because Steve was the lead architect for their firm on the Belzer project. "I'm not going to spy for you."

"Man, you owe me for letting you go to the conference in Denver so you could go rock climbing. Besides, this kind of thing goes on all the time."

Mark wavered. He didn't like the idea of trolling for information, but he couldn't deny the sudden compulsion to talk to Cassie again. Knowing his phone was getting ready to roll over to voice mail, he connected the call. "Hello?"

"Mark? Hi, it's Cassie…Goodwin."

She'd always had a great voice, so warm and sexy. False advertising, he noted wryly. "Hi, Cassie. What's up?"

"Busy, like always," she said breezily. "I'm on vacation doing some spring cleaning around my house today and found a couple of things that belong to you. I could drop them off at your office some time if you like."

Meaning, he didn't have to actually see her if he didn't want to. He glanced up to Steve, who rolled his hand in an encouraging gesture. Mark didn't plan to milk Cassie for information, but it gave him a cover to see her again. "Cassie, I'm in the field today. I could stop by your place this afternoon if you'll be around."

Steve gave him a thumbs-up.

"Okay, sure," she said. "It'll be great to see you."

He blinked. Had he imagined the note of flirtation in her voice? "You, too."

When he ended the call, he looked up to find Steve studying him. "Well?"

"Well…nothing," Mark said, setting aside the phone. "Cassie found some things at her place that belong to me. I'm going to pick them up."

Steve nodded. "A perfectly innocent excuse for you to poke around."

"Don't get your hopes up about me getting info on Ruger's bid. Cassie's no dummy."

"Hey, maybe she's calling you to try to get information about *our* bid."

Mark gave a little laugh. "You're wrong. This woman doesn't have a misbehaving bone in her body. Believe me, Cassie Goodwin has no ulterior motives for calling me."

CASSIE SET DOWN her phone and expelled a long, shaky breath. The call with Mark had actually gone better than she'd expected. She'd given him an out in case he truly didn't want to see her, but instead he'd offered to come by to pick up the mislaid items. Just hearing Mark's voice sent a shiver over her shoulders. On one hand, she was glad the reunion would take place on her turf. On the other hand…she didn't know what to do next.

Cassie picked up her phone and scrolled through her

contact list until she came to Red Tote Book Club. She needed help. Cassie texted Meeting ex bf in few minutes; advice? and sent it to the group. Hopefully someone would get her message in time to respond.

A few seconds later, her phone chimed. Cassie picked it up and smiled to see a note from Page Sharpe—Page was the quietest woman in the group, and the last person Cassie expected to hear from.

C—what would Lady Chatterley do?

Cassie pursed her mouth and nodded. Good guidance. On the table next to the phone lay a copy of *Lady Chatterley's Lover* by D. H. Lawrence, the book that had inspired Cassie to take control of her sex life. She picked up the book and flipped through the pages, skimming some of her favorite scenes featuring Connie Chatterley and the gamekeeper Mellors. If Connie Chatterley lived in this modern day and age and Mellors was coming over, what would Connie do?

In one scene after spotting Mellors, Connie had stripped in front of a mirror and studied her body, analyzing which parts of it Mellors might find the most attractive if he were watching.

On impulse, Cassie turned to the full-length mirror in her bedroom and appraised her figure clad in faded low-rise jeans and a yellow T-shirt. She was of average height and weight, with a figure that had always been a bit too curvy to be fashionable. But Mark had commented more than once that he wasn't attracted to women who were "a bag of bones."

Slowly, Cassie began to disrobe.

She lifted her T-shirt over her head, then reached around to unhook her sensible bra. Her breasts fell forward, the tips budding in the coolness of the air. They felt heavy with need. Every thought of Mark fueled her desire to seduce him, to let him know what he'd missed out on.

She unzipped her jeans and shimmied them down her legs, along with her practical, full-coverage panties. Cassie stared at her nude body from all angles. Her hips were generous, but shapely and firm, and her waist was tapered. Her legs and arms were slender and toned with the demands of her job, which often required her to be on a job site, hefting tools and coordinating equipment.

For thirty, she didn't look so bad naked, she decided with a lift of her chin. She had nothing to be ashamed of.

She started to redress, then paused and considered her beige underwear. It was rather…matronly. She walked to her bureau and rummaged to the back of a drawer until her fingers closed around the scrap of red lace she was looking for.

But the plain yellow T-shirt wasn't that sexy… unless she went braless.

And the jeans… Cassie reached for a pair of scissors.

She couldn't take a chance that Mark wouldn't notice her when he arrived.

She'd have to make sure he had plenty to look at.

3

FROM THE CURB, CASSIE'S refurbished ranch house was exactly as Mark remembered it. The woman had good taste, having removed all the extraneous detail added by previous owners, stripping the house to its original lines and low-to-the-ground profile. Although his personal style was more contemporary, he admired the mid-century design. Another example of how compatible he and Cassie had been...on every level except the one that mattered most. He reminded himself that by breaking it off when he had, he'd simply saved them both from a tedious situation that was headed straight for the "average" side of the relationship scale.

He parked his SUV in her driveway and climbed out, experiencing a mingling of familiarity and surprise at the things that had changed, the things he'd missed. Cassie's minimalist landscaping had gone through a growth spurt. And she'd painted her door a deep rust red that contrasted nicely with the gray wood siding.

He loosened his tie in the summer heat, rang the doorbell and waited, but there was no answer. Thinking Cassie might have moved to the outside in her cleaning, he decided to walk around to the backyard. Whistling lightly, he strolled around the side of the house. Sure enough, he heard the sound of a water hose. When he reached the gate leading to the backyard, he peeked around to get her attention…and froze.

Cassie was washing the exterior windows with a water hose, but had managed to soak herself in the process. Her dark ponytail sagged with moisture, and water dripped from her elbows. Her yellow T-shirt had molded to her breasts and it was clear she wasn't wearing a bra. Cut-off jean shorts hugged her wet thighs, revealing a generous length of toned leg.

Damn.

Mark's body reacted just as she looked up and noticed him. Her sunny smile hit him hard and he wondered briefly how he'd managed to get along without it all these months.

Cassie waved him inside the gate, then reached to turn off the water hose. Mark tried to maintain his composure as he walked closer, but he couldn't stop staring at her breasts, perfectly outlined in the wet T-shirt. And the more he stared, the tighter his pants got.

"Hi," Cassie called cheerfully, obviously unaware of the erotic picture she presented, standing there holding a hose, no less.

"Hi," Mark offered past a constricted throat. "Is this a bad time?"

"No, this is fine," she said. "I was just getting ready to take a break. Would you like a glass of lemonade?"

Since his mouth was dry and he was suddenly perspiring profusely, he said, "Sure."

"Come on in."

He followed Cassie toward the back door, so mesmerized by the swing of her rear end in the cut-off shorts that when she stopped and bent over to slip off her shoes, he bumped into her. Worse, he knocked her off balance and had to grasp her waist to keep her from falling. In the intimate dance, he was certain she felt his erection, and the feel of her rounded derriere only made things worse.

"I'm sorry," he said, flustered, but she only laughed it off and preceded him into the house. He followed her to the kitchen where they'd made several good meals together, he recalled. He frowned. Why did he keep remembering all the things they had in common?

"So what have you been up to lately?" Cassie asked as she turned her back to remove two glasses from the cupboard.

"Same old," he said casually.

"Any interesting projects on the horizon?"

Mark opened his mouth to respond, but whatever he'd been about to say flew out of his head when Cassie opened the refrigerator door and leaned over. The short shorts rode up, revealing toned hamstrings…and the edge of lacy red panties. His cock expanded farther.

She straightened and turned, holding the lemonade. The chill of the fridge had turned her nipples to hardened points, poking through the T-shirt. "Nothing?"

Mark blinked. "Huh?"

She laughed. "Interesting projects?"

He thought of the Belzer job. "Not really. How about you?"

"A few things," she said vaguely. "I took off today because things are about to get busy."

She poured them each a glass of lemonade, and when she lifted her glass, her pink tongue flicked out to catch a drop on the rim. Mark stared, captivated, then drank deeply from his own glass, hoping the cold liquid would help to cool him down. "I saw that Rugers is bidding on the Belzer Tower project."

Cassie nodded. "I'm heading up the bid."

His pulse jumped. "So you'll be lead architect?"

"If we get the job. I saw your firm on the list, too."

He nodded.

She smiled. "I guess it's a good thing we aren't seeing each other anymore, or that could be sticky."

He gave a little laugh and nodded.

"Oh—here are your things." From the end of the counter she picked up a folded shirt and handed it to him, then dropped a pair of silver cufflinks in his hand.

Mark unfolded the Atlanta Motor Speedway T-shirt that was easily an XXL and pursed his mouth. "Uh… this isn't my shirt."

Cassie's eyes went wide. "Are you sure?"

He gave her a wry smile. "Yeah. The owner of this shirt is a lot bigger than me."

"Really?" She took the shirt and held it up to his chest, as if she needed proof. The warmth of her fingers burned through the fabric to his skin. Then she frowned at the overhang and bit her lip, as if she were trying to remember to whom it belonged. Finally, she shrugged and set the shirt aside. "But the cufflinks are yours?"

He uncurled his fingers to look at the smart, modern cubic design. And they weren't silver as he'd first thought—they were platinum. "Nice, but…no, these aren't mine either."

A little frown crossed her brow. "Are you sure?"

"I'm sure." He handed them back to her. "Actually, I don't remember ever getting undressed here."

She looked confused for a moment, as if she couldn't recall.

Mark frowned—she couldn't remember that they hadn't slept together? It certainly loomed large enough in his memory.

Then her plump mouth formed an O. "That's right," she said, nodding. "Now I remember." Cassie carefully set the cufflinks on the counter. "Sorry to make you drive all the way over here for nothing."

"That's all right," Mark said smoothly. "It was nice to see you again."

"You, too," she said with that smile that made his stomach clench. Then she pushed away from the counter. "Well, I guess I'd better get back to my cleaning and let you get back to work."

He set his empty glass on the counter and followed her outside, suddenly loathe to leave. He told himself it was because he hadn't gotten any helpful info on the Belzer project. "Is there something I can give you a hand with?"

"Not at the moment, but if I come up against a job I need your muscles for, can I give you a call?"

Her compliment warmed him and inadvertently his shoulders went back. "Sure."

She followed him to the gate. Mark hesitated, then cleared his throat. "Um, Cassie, listen. I'm really sorry about the way things ended between us."

She nodded. "Me, too. But you were right—something was missing. I think it's important that two people have chemistry, don't you?"

He nodded absently, distracted by the chemical reaction straining his zipper. "Right. Well, I guess I'd better go."

"Bye, now."

He drank in one last look at her moist T-shirt and exited the gate to walk around to his SUV.

Mark climbed behind the wheel and puffed out his cheeks in an exhale.

So maybe Cassie Goodwin wasn't the prude he thought she was. Apparently she'd been entertaining a big strapping professional with good taste in cufflinks and who enjoyed motor sports.

Then he frowned. Assuming the items belonged to the same guy.

Mark shifted in his seat. He'd assumed that Cassie had been a cold fish…but maybe she just hadn't been interested in *him*. The thought rankled him—he was a sexy guy…wasn't he?

As he pulled away from the curb, his phone rang. The caller ID showed it was Steve calling.

Mark flipped open the phone. "Yeah, Steve."

"Did you get anything on the Belzer project?"

"Just that Cassie's handling the bid for Rugers."

"Perfect," Steve said. "You're going to call her again, right?"

Mark glanced in his rear view mirror. Cassie was back to window washing, straddling a step ladder. Mark had never been envious of an inanimate object before. "Uh…yeah, I'm going to call her again."

CASSIE WATCHED MARK drive away out of the corner of her eye. Her heart pumped wildly. Had pretending that her brother's T-shirt and cufflinks belonged to a lover worked? Had she piqued Mark's interest, given him a glimpse of what he'd missed?

From the clip on her waistband, her phone rang. She glanced at the screen and gave a little squeal to see Mark's name. Cassie connected the call. "Hello?"

"Cassie, hi. It's Mark."

"Did you decide to lay claim to the cufflinks?" she teased.

He gave a little laugh. "No. Actually, my team could use a fourth in a charity golf scramble this Saturday afternoon at Trembley. Would you be interested?"

Cassie smiled into the phone. It wasn't exactly a rendezvous in the woods, like Connie and Mellors in *Lady Chatterley's Lover*, but it was a chance to spend time with him in the outdoors. And his invitation meant that her seduction plan was working—he was thinking about her. "Sure, that sounds like fun."

"Okay. See you then."

She disconnected the call and put a hand over her racing heart. Seeing Mark again had affected her more than she'd expected—she'd forgotten how tall he was, and how handsome. The juxtaposition of earthy male in shirt and tie had her body on full alert, throbbing to a beat entirely separate from her pulse.

Suddenly, Cassie was bombarded with text messages from her book club members.

How did it go?
Did he take the bait?
Details, details.
Is the seduction under way?

Cassie used her thumbs to type in Everything going as planned....

4

"ARE YOU SURE she's coming?" Steve asked, leaning on his golf clubs. "Just our luck that Thomson has the flu."

Mark gave his coworker a wry smile. "Somehow I think Thomson got the worse end of things."

"We'll be disqualified if we don't have at least three players."

"Relax. Cassie said she'd be here." Mark's admonishment was more for himself than for his antsy partner. Since earlier in the week, the image of her wet T-shirt and short shorts had worn on his nerves like a file. And inexplicably, the good times they'd shared seemed to rise from the recesses of his memory to taunt him. He missed talking with someone who understood the demands and frustrations of his job. He missed her easy smile and quick laugh. He missed wondering what she was hiding under her shapeless clothes, and why.

And he'd left without giving her a chance to reveal either.

"Are you okay?" Steve asked. "You look like you ate bad potato salad."

"I'm fine. When Cassie gets here, don't mention the Belzer project—let me handle it."

"Okay, this is all on you. You know what we have

riding on this bid." Suddenly Steve straightened. "Yowza. Now *that's* a nice set of legs."

Mark followed his coworker's line of sight to the path above them leading to the tee. A set of lean, tanned legs came into view and Mark's pulse jerked in recognition. "That's Cassie."

Steve's eyebrows shot up as the rest of her came into view. "I don't remember her looking like that."

Mark was torn between feeling protective and being irritated—he didn't remember her looking like that, either.

She had traded her traditional chinos and baggy polo shirt for a navy blue athletic skirt and a white sleeveless shirt, both of which fit her hourglass figure like a glove. Her dark hair was scooped back from her face with a yellow visor, her ponytail bobbing in time with her quick, confident stride. Instead of using a pull-cart, she had shouldered her golf clubs, and carried them with athletic ease. When Cassie saw Mark, she waved and her lovely face lit up with a smile.

"Why did you break up with her again?" Steve asked, still staring. "I thought you said she wasn't sexy."

Mark frowned. "With your golf handicap, you really should try to keep your eye on the ball today."

"It's a scramble," Steve muttered. "Only one of the three of us has to play well. Besides, what's the harm in looking? It's not as if you're interested in her. You dumped her, remember?"

A sour mood descended over Mark, but he managed a smile when Cassie came bouncing up like a ball of sunshine.

"Am I late?" she asked.

"Right on time," Steve said smoothly, then extended his hand.

Mark had to stop himself from rolling his eyes. "Cassie Goodwin, meet my coworker, Steve Hamlin."

"Hi," she said, meeting his hand.

Mark noticed that she didn't seem to mind that Steve held on longer than necessary. The XXL shirt and the cufflinks popped into his mind. The fact that Cassie had had at least one overnight guest since their breakup meant she was open to male companionship. Steve and Cassie fell into step, heading toward the first tee where other golfers had gathered. Mark followed behind, watching their interplay with growing ire.

What was it about him that Cassie had retreated from? Had he been insensitive? Pushy? Unromantic?

All of the above?

Adding to his foul mood, of their threesome, only Cassie seemed to be able to focus on the game. He and Steve both were so distracted by her, Cassie had the best shot on the first two holes.

"Nice swing," Steve said under his breath, but he was staring at her ass, not her club.

"Knock it off," Mark said irritably.

"What are you, her boyfriend?" Steve said under his breath, then raised his voice when Cassie approached them. "So, Cassie—I hear that you and Mark used to date."

She smiled at Mark. "That's right."

"So tell me something about my friend here that I don't know."

Mark shifted uncomfortably under her gaze. *That*

I'm a jerk for breaking things off the way I did. That I was thinking with the wrong head. That I didn't give us a chance.

"He gives great back rubs," Cassie said, her blue eyes full of mirth.

"You don't say?" Steve turned raised eyebrows in Mark's direction.

Mark gave a tight smile, but inside he was perplexed. He'd never given Cassie a backrub—she obviously had him confused with some other guy who had his hands all over her.

And why did the thought of some other guy having his hands all over Cassie arouse such strong feelings of jealousy?

During the rest of the nine-hole scramble, Mark was torn between wanting the event to end, yet enjoying the chance to study Cassie unobserved. Her concentration was intense. She wrinkled her nose adorably just before she swung the club. And her neck…how had he never noticed the elegant line of her neck?

"Man, we're almost done and I haven't heard you mention Belzer," Steve whispered.

"I told you, I'll handle it," Mark returned.

Steve elbowed him. "Back rub, huh? You sly dog. I thought you said you didn't sleep with her."

Anger rose in his chest. "Drop it, Steve."

His coworker lifted his hands. "Whatever you say."

By the time they finished playing and picked up the third-place trophy—thanks to Cassie's great game— Mark was eager to be alone with her. He followed her to the parking lot, as nervous as a teenager, trying to make small talk. Desperate, he fell back on the only subject that came to mind. "How's the bid for the Belzer project going?"

She gave him a suspicious glance. "Fine. Why?"

He attempted a casual shrug, but guilt stabbed at him. "Just making conversation. Hey, I didn't realize you were such a good golfer."

"Maybe you don't know everything about me," she returned lightly.

At her subtle reference to a sensual side of her he hadn't bothered to get to know, his cock twitched.

"Oh, no," Cassie said, stopping in front of her small SUV. "I left my lights on. I hope my battery isn't dead." She opened the door and slid behind the wheel. When she turned the key, a clicking noise sounded. "It's dead, alright."

"I'll give you a jump," Mark offered quickly.

She glanced up at him, a sexy smile curving her mouth.

Mark felt like an idiot. "I mean…I'll give your battery a jump…with my car…of course."

Cassie laughed. "I'd appreciate it."

Mark carried his golf clubs to his vehicle, and gave himself a mental shake. Women didn't normally throw him off balance, and certainly not women that he'd—as Steve had so eloquently put it—*dumped*. But being around Cassie made him think maybe he'd made a mistake ending their relationship. He'd always thought she was a great person and a talented architect. He enjoyed her company. He'd only been disappointed in her apparent disinterest in sex. But apparently he hadn't been very observant.

Lost in thought, he pulled his vehicle across the lot to her SUV. Cassie had already lifted the hood and was leaning in to connect jumper cables to her dead battery. The navy sport skirt rode high on the backs of her tanned, toned thighs, eliciting thoughts of her bent over, naked, opening herself to receive him.

Mark groaned as a powerful lust surged through his body. He had to have her, to see what he'd missed. But the question was, would Cassie give him another chance?

CASSIE STEPPED BACK FROM her car and nearly bumped into Mark, who had walked up behind her. His nearness sent her pulse rocketing. Desire stabbed her deep in her womb. Her sex was already primed and sensitive from watching him all day…and knowing that he was watching her.

He held up a golf towel. "Thought you might want to wipe your hands."

"Thank you," she said, taking it.

She watched as he lifted the hood of his vehicle and connected the other end of the jumper cables to his battery. The muscles in his bronze arms bunched, giving her a little thrill. What would it be like to lie in his strong arms, skin to skin?

"I'll start my engine," he said, then they exchanged a look before he climbed into his vehicle.

Suddenly everything they said seemed laden with innuendo. Cassie felt silly and young and flush with the hope that they could explore this burgeoning chemistry between them. A few minutes later, he signaled her to turn over her engine. She did, and thankfully, it engaged.

Mark got out and disconnected the cables, then lowered the car hoods and came around to her window. "Let your engine idle for a few minutes to charge the battery. I'll follow you home to make sure everything is okay."

"That's not necessary," she protested.

"I want to." His eyes flashed with the heat of a protector. "Since you showed me up on the golf course, at least let me save face by doing something manly."

She laughed. "Okay. Thanks."

Seeing Mark in her rearview mirror all the way home made her feel warm and feminine. She pulled into the garage and parked, then to calm her pounding heart, she pulled up the list she'd made on her phone. *Invent reasons to cross paths...make yourself available...be secretive...be naughty...surprise him.*

After a few deep breaths, she jumped out and walked back to his SUV. "Everything's fine. Thanks again." *Surprise him.*

"No prob—"

Cassie cut him off with a searing kiss. She opened her mouth and thrust her tongue against his in a slow, sensual match, tasting him and sighing into his mouth. When she pulled back, she was gratified to see the kiss had had the intended effect.

"—lem," he finished, then his Adam's apple bobbed. "Wow. I don't remember..."

She angled her head. "Don't remember what?"

"Never mind. But I'm curious—why did you tell Steve I gave good back rubs?"

She grinned. "Because I have a good imagination." She pushed away from the SUV and waved. "I had fun today—thanks for asking me to play."

Then she bounded toward her house, feeling confident she'd given him something to think about.

That evening her fellow members of the Red Tote Book Club texted her.

How's it going?
Update please.
Don't keep us in suspense.
Have you sealed the deal?

She smiled, then texted back Got him on a slow burn....

The only problem, she admitted when she put down the phone, was that she was about ready to combust herself. She bit her lip and asked herself what Connie Chatterley would do and decided that Connie would take matters into her own hands, so to speak. But when it came to seduction, timing was everything....

5

MARK WIPED THE SWEAT off his neck, but cursed at the return of the persistent throb in his shorts. A six-mile run hadn't been enough to eradicate the thought of Cassie Goodwin from his mind. The wet T-shirt...the sight of her tanned thighs...that slip of a skirt...

He groaned and entered his condo building, then took the stairs two at a time to his unit on the fifth floor. He never tired of its clean lines and modern décor, but lately it felt a little...sterile. Lonely, even. He stripped his clothes on the way to the bathroom, eager to get into a shower. After rinsing under the coldest water he could withstand, he stepped out and wrapped a towel around his waist. Feeling somewhat better, he padded to his den to pour a drink and boot up his laptop. Predictably, he had an e-mail from Steve.

Have you found out anything about Rugers' bid on the Belzer project? A sneak peek at their site plan could give us a leg up, considering our excavators are giving us mixed feedback as to the best way to proceed.

Mark pulled his hand down his face. He wanted to ask Cassie out on a real date, but he'd decided to wait a couple of weeks until the bid for the Belzer project had been awarded. Then neither of them could be accused of impropriety.

And considering how much she'd been on his mind the last couple of days, that day couldn't come soon enough. As he sipped bourbon from his glass, his phone rang. He sighed, assuming it was Steve, but when he glanced at the caller ID and saw Cassie's name, he immediately connected the call.

"Hello," he said, trying not to sound too eager.

"Hi, it's Cassie. Did I catch you at a bad time?"

He closed his eyes—oh, that voice. "Hi, Cassie. No, I'm just—" *Sitting here thinking about you.* "Working on the Belzer project. What are you up to?"

Her laugh tinkled over the line. "Nothing quite so impressive. I'd like to order a chair, but before I do, I wondered if your offer of muscle is still open."

He unconsciously flexed his biceps. "Sure."

"Great. The chair won't be delivered until next week, but they're going to drop ship it to the curb, and I'll need help to get it up to my bedroom."

Bedroom? His cock twitched. "No problem. Just let me know when you come." He winced. "I mean… when it comes."

"Okay. Thanks, Mark. I really appreciate it. I'm so glad that we can be friends now. Bye."

Mark tried to think of something to extend the conversation, but was too thrown by her comment about them being friends to react quickly enough. Friends? He didn't want to be *friends* with Cassie. Of course, considering he'd dumped her, being friends was a gracious offer on her behalf.

When he started to disconnect the call, he frowned at the noise on the other end of the line. It sounded as if Cassie had set down the phone without ending the call. In the background, he could hear her moving around, humming. He started to call her name, but he conceded he liked the idea of listening to her happy sounds, and it dawned on him that he wished he was there with her. He imagined her bustling around, smiling at nothing and everything, unsuspecting of how outrageously sexy she was.

Then the humming grew louder and he realized with a start it was mechanical, not human. An electric toothbrush maybe?

But when Cassie's moan sounded in the background, he blinked. No way...she wasn't...

"Ummm...ummm...oh..."

She was using a vibrator to masturbate. Despite his incredulity, Mark's cock began to thicken. Instantly he pictured her lying on the bed, naked, her knees open, stroking her clit with the vibrator. He reached under the towel covering him and grasped his hardening length. God, he wanted to be there, plying her with his tongue until she tossed out the battery-operated contraption.

How did she taste? Probably like her kiss—honey and musk, intoxicating. His mouth watered for her.

He stroked himself in time with her moans and gasps, so caught up in her sensuous noises that he almost dropped the phone. He kept his mouth away from the receiver so she wouldn't hear his own panting. His balls began to tingle and he knew he was very close to losing control. He slowed, taking his cues from her soft murmurings. When her cries began to climb, he followed pace. And when she shouted her release with a passion that shocked him, he joined in her climax, shooting his load with a guttural groan.

He shared in the breathlessness of her recovery, then he reluctantly disconnected the call, lest she realized what she'd done. Shaken, he sat up and drank deeply from his glass. He'd never imagined that Cassie Goodwin was the kind of woman who...pleasured herself.

Then a disturbing thought occurred to him—who had she been thinking about while she fondled herself? Mr. XXL, or maybe Mr. Platinum Cufflinks?

Certainly not the man who had dumped her, he acknowledged morosely.

But he so wanted it to be him.

6

CASSIE WAS DECIDEDLY NERVOUS when Mark pulled into her driveway. It had been over a week since her "accidental" self-gratification incident. Judging from the timestamp of the length of the call, he'd heard everything before hanging up. But the fact that he hadn't called her in the days since made her uneasy.

Had he been repulsed by her behavior? He had seemed so attentive to her when he'd dropped by her house, and on the golf course, and so responsive to her heated kiss, but maybe she'd gone too far.

Or maybe he was seeing someone else, she reasoned. After all, it seemed likely that the handsome, successful architect would have his pick of girlfriends. Or maybe he truly just wasn't into her, as his parting words from their previous breakup had insinuated.

If so, she admitted, standing next to the giant crate delivered to the curb, this could very well be the most humiliating experience of her life. She'd have to find a new book club because she'd have to move to another city.

Mark climbed out of his SUV looking impossibly fit and handsome in worn jeans and a pale blue T-shirt that set off his hazel eyes. Just the sight of him set her heart in motion. She was still in love with him, she realized with a sinking sensation, which only made this more risky. For a few seconds, she considered bailing and telling him the manufacturer had sent the wrong piece of furniture. But then she remembered the words of the book club coordinator, Gabrielle.

I don't want you to be alone when you're pushing forty, like me, and asking yourself 'what if?'

Cassie took a deep breath for courage. She didn't want that for herself either, to look back and ask what if she'd let Mark Shapiro see the sexy side of her she hadn't been able to show anyone else? She wanted to be able to say that she'd revealed all of herself, even the side that she was still getting used to. If Mark rejected her again, then so be it, but it wouldn't be because she held back.

"Hi," he said.

His smile and admiring glance over her jeans and tank top gave her a shot of encouragement. Were her cheeks as red as they felt? "Hi, Mark. You're a dear to come and help me like this."

He ran a hand over the edge of the large crate. "This must be a good size chair."

She wet her lips. "It is."

"Okay." He picked up the crowbar she'd removed from the garage. "Let's get it uncrated."

She stood back as he pried off the side panel of the crate. Inside, the chair was obscured by wood shavings and bubble wrap. She helped him lift the long, horizontal shape from the crate.

"That's a funny-looking chair," he remarked.

Her pulse jumped. "Actually, it's part chair, part bench."

"Okay, well, I think I can get it if you'll hold open the door and show me where you want it."

She walked ahead of him as he wielded the awkward piece of furniture, opening doors and clearing the way to her bedroom. When he crossed the threshold, she pointed to an empty corner of the room. "You can set it there."

He lowered the item to the floor carefully, then straightened and glanced all around her room, his gaze lingering on the mid-century style bed of pale maple. Just the sight of Mark inside her austere bedroom made her stomach flip. She'd pointed it out to him when she'd given him the initial tour of her home, but he'd never slept over, never spent any time at all in her room.

He gestured to the wrapped chair. "Don't I at least get to see it?"

She smiled and nodded, then retrieved a pair of scissors. But her hand shook slightly as she cut away the tape and packing material to reveal the long contoured, armless chaise-like chair upholstered in supple black matte leather. It was higher on one end, with a deep dip in the center.

He scratched his head. "That's an interesting design, but it looks…comfortable."

Cassie took a deep breath, then announced. "It's a tantric chair."

He looked confused, then his eyebrows rose. "Tantric, as in…sex?"

She nodded, holding his gaze.

His mouth opened slightly, then his eyes went smoky. "If you're trying to torture me, Cassie, it's working."

The air between them sizzled with electricity. His body language—the softening of his eyes, the hardening of his jaw, the bulge in his pants—told her how much he wanted her. But the clenching of his hands meant he was holding back, hoping she would make the first move?

It was the moment before Connie Chatterley marched into Mellors's cabin in the woods and lay down on his bed.

It was now or never, Cassie realized.

She closed the space between them and looped her arms around Mark's neck. "Do you know what I'm thinking?"

A muscle worked in his jaw. "Not a clue."

"I'm thinking we never had break-up sex."

He nodded carefully, as if he was afraid to break the moment. "Actually, we never had any kind of sex."

She raised on her toes and whispered, "So, do you want to break in the chair?"

7

MARK'S EARS RANG. Had he heard Cassie correctly? Did he want to help her break in her sex chair? The blood supply to his brain was restricted as it suddenly rushed to priority areas of his body.

"Absolutely," he said on an exhale, then pulled her against him in a powerful, ravenous kiss. He devoured her mouth and cupped her hips against his, their hands sliding up and down each other's body. Cassie tugged on the hem of his T-shirt and lifted it over his head. He fumbled with the buttons on her shirt until she was free of it. The sight of the white lacy bra containing her generous breasts sent his erection surging against his zipper. Even as his frenzied hands separated her from her jeans, Mark told himself to slow down, that he wanted their first time to be special, to be memorable. When Cassie reached for his zipper, he stilled her hands.

"Not yet. I want this to last for you."

He lifted her and set her on the high end of the chair, kissing her deeply while unhooking her bra. When her breasts spilled into his hands, Mark thought he might lose control on the spot. High and firm, with cotton-candy pink nipples against tanned skin, they were magnificent. He laved the puffy nipples, drawing them into his mouth until she cried out in pleasure. He rolled the tiny panties down her long, slender legs as he gently guided her to lie down the length of the bench, leaving her head slightly lower, her back arched, and her sex open to him.

Her essence was so heady, he had to set his jaw in restraint. Then he lowered his tongue to the dark curls at the juncture of her thighs. Her cry of surprise and delight reverberated off the walls of her bedroom as her legs tensed around his shoulders. He stroked up and down her folds, then latched on to the tiny nub at the core of her pleasure and sucked gently.

Cassie thought she was going to die from pure ecstasy. The sensations bombarding her were like nothing she'd ever experienced…the fact that it was Mark making love to her with his mouth made it almost unbearable. A vibration deep inside her belly signaled the onset of a powerful orgasm. Her muscles twitched and her body convulsed as the climax worked its way to the surface, and when she rocketed over the edge and flew into a thousand pieces, she thought it was only right to call out his name because he had given her the most wonderful physical experience of her life. "Mark…oh, Mark…Mark."

She was so drained afterward, she had to cling to the chair. Above her, through the frame of her knees, Mark stood and fumbled with his zipper, then freed his erection. He pulled out his wallet, removed a condom, then tossed the wallet aside. He was panting as he sheathed himself, his eyes hooded. Cassie opened her knees to welcome him. He gripped her buttocks and entered her with one long thrust. Cassie gasped at the sensation of him filling her, stretching her. She wrapped her legs around his waist and met his thrusts, each one more exhilarating than the last. When the bliss reached the point of almost unbearable, he drove deep and shuddered against her, murmuring against her knees. When he gasped her name, she brimmed with satisfaction, knowing she had given him the same gift he'd given her. When he fell forward and ran his hands down her naked body, then intertwined their fingers, Cassie was infused with love.

She closed her eyes and remembered that Lady Chatterley's love affair had started magically and ended tragically. She pushed the thought aside.

WHEN MARK JERKED AWAKE, his face was buried in strawberry-scented hair. He smiled in realization that he was in Cassie's bed, and allowed the memories of the previous night to rush over him. They had enjoyed every position the wonderful sex chair had allowed them to achieve. His body ached pleasantly from their erotic exertion, and he had no feeling in his arm curled beneath Cassie. But it was the vaguely unsettling sensation in his chest that most concerned him.

He rolled to his back and gently extracted his arm. Cassie rolled over to face him and sighed happily before her breathing deepened again into sleep. Rosy, predawn light fell on her face. When he took in the sweep of her dark lashes against her cheeks and the tilt of her nose, the bud of her pink mouth, the truth hit him like a two by four: He could love this woman. She was everything he could ever want in a partner, and more passionate than he could've imagined.

Even now, when they were sated and sore, he wanted her again, wanted to join with her body and look into her intelligent blue eyes and see himself reflected a better man. He felt humbled that she had come back into his life.

"I think I love you," he whispered to her sleeping form.

Her breathing hitched, then resumed.

An involuntary smile lifted his mouth as pure happiness and optimism flowed through his chest. He was already looking forward to when they could be together again. They would have to keep a low profile until the bid for the Belzer project was announced next week, then they could make their relationship public.

Mark turned his head to check the clock on the nightstand. He had to be at an industry breakfast in an hour. With reluctance and as quietly as possible, he eased from her bed and gathered his clothes as he left her bedroom. He stepped into the open area of her home office to redress. It was a neat, well-proportioned workspace, with her drafting table placed under a southern facing skylight. His mind raced ahead, thinking how they might fit two drafting tables in the space…or maybe they would get a new place together.

Then his gaze landed on the thick folder lying on the table. The label identified its contents as the Belzer Tower project. Inside was likely everything that Steve wanted to know. Mark swallowed hard, then stumbled backward in his hurry to get away from it.

He let himself out the front door, buoyed by the thought that someday soon he could loiter in bed with Cassie.

WHEN CASSIE'S EYES POPPED open, she smiled into her pillow as memories from the previous evening flowed over her like a sensuous waterfall. She smoothed her hand over the indention Mark's head had left in his pillow, then she stretched and squealed with pure joy. Her body was tender in all the right places. During the night she had experienced physical heights she hadn't known existed. She wished she could lie in bed all day and steep in the feeling of being in love, but a glance at the clock sent her catapulting out of bed.

She had to be at an industry breakfast in less than an hour.

After racing through a shower and dressing quickly, she grabbed the Belzer file from her drafting table, stuffed it in her briefcase, then ran out the door with a smile on her face. She and Mark would have to lie low until the winning firm was announced, but after that, they could go public with their relationship again.

And this time, things would be different, all because she'd dared to let him see a side of her that Gabrielle had encouraged her to reveal. A sensual side that Cassie didn't know she had until she read *Lady Chatterley's Lover*. She couldn't wait to report back to her book club members that she had been successful in seducing the man of her dreams. She'd told the group that she would be okay if the seduction didn't lead to a long-term relationship, but now she knew that she hadn't been honest with herself. She couldn't have been so sexually open with Mark if she hadn't already been in love with him.

But her love for him had bloomed overnight because of their intense physical chemistry.

She made it to the breakfast only a few minutes late,

but she was in such a good mood, she didn't care. On the way in, she spotted Mark in the foyer talking with someone, and her heart lifted crazily at the thought that only a few hours ago, he'd been in her bed.

She walked toward him to let him know she was there, but realized at the last second that he was talking to his coworker Steve Hamlin, the one who had ogled her on the golf course. Steve seemed agitated.

"Mark, we're coming down to the wire on the Belzer project. You said you were going to find out from your old flame what Rugers has in the game. Did you get the site plan or not?"

Cassie blinked, then cold, hard realization shot through her. Mark had asked her about the Belzer project a few times. Her work file had been lying on her drafting table this morning.

Her heart shivered at the dawning of the truth. Mark didn't have feelings for her. She had simply been a means to an end.

8

MARK OPENED HIS MOUTH to tell Steve to go to hell, but his friend suddenly blanched.

"Uh-oh."

When Mark looked over his shoulder and saw Cassie standing there, he shrank inside. From the expression on her face, she'd heard every word that Steve had said.

Her blue eyes shimmered with unshed tears. "The site plan for the Belzer project? That's why you've been hanging around?"

He put up his hands, as if he could piece back together what had just broken. "No. Let me explain."

Cassie leaned in. "Are you going to explain that the sex was just a bonus to you?"

His buddy Steve snickered. Mark turned back and shook his head, then made a fist and punched his coworker in the nose. Steve yelped and went flailing backward as blood spurted and people scrambled to clear out of his way.

When Mark turned back to Cassie, she was gone. He pivoted his head and spotted her hurrying toward the exit. He sprang into motion and ran after her.

"Cassie! Wait!" He caught up with her and reached for her arm, but she pulled away.

"Leave me alone, Mark. You've humiliated me twice now—I get it. You're just not into me."

"Please hear me out," he said. "That's all I ask before you walk away from us."

She stopped and crossed her arms, then lifted her hurt gaze to his expectantly.

Mark took a deep breath. "I only let Steve think I was going after information on the Belzer project because I didn't want to admit I was an idiot for letting you get away the first time." He sighed. "It was stupid, and I don't expect you to forgive me, but I want you to know that the only reason I was with you is because I wanted to be. I didn't even open the project file. I couldn't care less about that job." He pulled his hand over his mouth. "In fact, no matter what happens, I'll see to it myself that my firm withdraws from the bid."

Her expression was still skeptical. Her mouth flattened, then she turned to go.

Panic seized his lungs. His mind went into full tactical mode. With nothing else to lose, he blurted, "I love you."

Cassie stopped, and replayed the words in her head. Mark loved her? Was that possible? Her heart lifted and she chanced a look back to see if he was mocking her, or playing her. But the look on Mark's face was... tortured.

"I do," he repeated, his eyes earnest. "I love you, Cassie. I don't deserve it after blowing it twice, but please give me another chance."

She considered him, the man who had left her heart in limbo, the man who had prompted her to be honest about her own sexuality, the man who had opened her world with one night of lovemaking. When they had climaxed together, she understood the powerful feeling that Connie had felt for Mellors when their bodies had pinnacled together. It was formidable.

Mark looked anguished. His jaw hardened and he seemed to be holding his breath for her response. And just the realization that her answer meant so much to him answered her own question.

Finally, Cassie angled her head. "You don't look very happy for someone who's in love."

His smile was tentative and he gave a little laugh. "I am happy. At least I was this morning when I woke up."

"I was happy, too," she admitted.

He exhaled and looked heavenward in relief. Then he stepped closer and pulled her into his arms. He smoothed her hair back from her face. "I love you. Did I say that already?"

Cassie nodded up at him, her heart engorged. "I love you, too."

He lowered his mouth to hers for a thorough kiss, then lifted his head. "Do I want to know where you learned all the things you did to me last night?"

She smiled. "Between the covers of some great books."

"No kidding?" A grin crept up Mark's face. "Speaking of between the covers, let's get out of here. I suddenly have the urge to spend the day in bed."

Cassie clasped his hand and yanked him toward the exit.

TURNING THE PAGE

1

"PAGE—WAIT!"

At the sound of her name being called, Page Sharpe winced and turned back at the threshold of the office of Armstrong Enterprises. Jessica Shepherd stood there, all six feet of her blondness, looking like a fashion model in her designer skirt suit, impeccably groomed.

"Yes?" Page asked, feeling every inch the frump.

Jessica strode up and extended an envelope. "Richard and I need this to be overnighted."

Page tamped down her anger. Having been the personal assistant of the senior Mr. Armstrong who had died suddenly eight months ago, she had seniority over Jessica, yet somehow the woman managed to categorize herself with their now-shared boss, Richard Armstrong, and make Page feel like the underling.

"I'm sorry," Page said, "but I can't. I'm running late as it is."

Jessica frowned. "Where do *you* have to be?"

Page set her jaw at the woman's inference that Page couldn't possibly have anywhere important to go. "My book club meets tonight."

Jessica gave her the once over, scanning Page's plaited red hair, long, baggy dress and flat shoes with thinly veiled disdain. "You belong to a book club? Shocker." The woman plunked the package into Page's arms. "Sorry, bookworm, but you're going to be a little late for tea and crumpets. This has to go out."

Page bit her lip. "Why can't you do it?"

"Because Richard asked me to ask *you* to do it." A smug smile pulled at the woman's mouth. "I have to stay and help Richard with something important."

Jessica turned on her heel and walked back into their boss's office. Page craned her neck for a glimpse of Richard. He was seated behind his enormous desk, his dark head bent over documents spread all over the surface, his tie loose, and his expression harried. He'd worked nonstop since his father's death, covering all aspects of the venture capital firm the elder Mr. Armstrong had built. She worried about the toll the increased workload was taking on Richard's health. He looked as if he had the weight of the world on his broad shoulders. Page's heart thudded wildly until the closing of the office door cut him off from her line of sight.

Then she glanced at the package in her hand and heaved a sigh. If Richard needed for her to drop off a package for overnight delivery, then she would. She'd do anything for the man who had so adored and admired his father.

Yet she hated being late for the Red Tote Book Club because she wanted to hear if one of her fellow members had been able to finish the assignment their coordinator, Gabrielle, had given to the group: To take the lessons they'd learned from the books of erotic literature they had read over the past few months and apply them to seduce the man of their dreams.

Putting words into action, so to speak.

Page hurried to her car and set the package on the passenger seat next to the red canvas tote bag she'd bought to hold the special books they read in the book club. The women in the group would never know how much their camaraderie meant to her, to be able to talk openly about sex without feeling judged. And now this exciting new challenge that had dominated her thoughts since their leader had proposed it. Page gave a little laugh because the idea of her seducing a man seemed about as plausible as her conquering Mt. Everest. She dreamed of exciting affairs as much as the next woman, but it only took one look in the mirror to recognize her limitations. She would, most likely, remain a spectator to this particular exercise.

Mentally calculating the nearest overnight package drop-off facility, she dutifully drove there, stood in line to fill out the appropriate forms, and watched as the precious package was taken away. When she finally wheeled into the parking lot of the branch of the Atlanta Public Library where the Red Tote Book Club met, she was twenty minutes late. They'd surely started without her, maybe even thought she'd dropped out.

As Page reached for her tote bag, which also held a container of homemade brownies—her contribution to the treats they shared each month—her cell phone rang. She sighed, but when she glanced at the caller ID to see the name RICHARD ARMSTRONG, she gasped and connected the call. "Yes, Mr. Armstrong?"

"Page," he said, his voice deep and husky, "I've asked you a hundred times to call me Richard."

She swallowed hard. "Yes…Richard?"

"I'm sorry to bother you. I understand you have a book club meeting tonight?"

Her face burned—she could only imagine Jessica telling Richard about Page's "boring" little pastime. They'd probably had a big laugh at her expense. "That's right," she murmured.

"That sounds nice," he said, his voice warm and sincere. "I won't keep you. I just wanted to thank you for taking the package to the courier."

"It's my job," she said a little breathlessly.

"You're good at your job," he said. "You make my life easier."

She was so flattered, she didn't know how to respond.

"I'll see you tomorrow," he said. "Goodnight, Page."

"Goodnight...Richard," she said on an exhale. She disconnected the call slowly, thrilled to her toes. It wasn't much of a conversation, but the act of him calling her after working hours had a whiff of intimacy that she clung to. She closed her eyes and smiled to herself.

"Goodnight, Richard," Page whispered, just for her own ears, imagining they were together in a more private setting. She has been infatuated with him since the day she'd first joined the firm as his father's assistant. He was breathtakingly handsome, no doubt. But working under his father, who talked so affectionately and proudly of Richard, had fostered her feelings for the son to deep admiration. And when she'd observed how Richard had revered his father, it only made her like him more. In fact, she was more than a little in love with him.

On his part, Richard had never given her more than a passing glance or a cordial nod and small talk around the coffeepot. She treasured every word he spared in her direction. And she only wished she had the power to affect him the way he affected her.

Remembering she was late, Page's eyes popped open and she sprang into motion.

Her mind was working even faster than her feet, turning over an idea that she'd dreamed of, fantasized about, but hadn't dared put into words…yet with the unexpected phone call, it was gaining momentum in her frenzied mind.

The room in the library where the Red Tote Book Club met was down a labyrinth of hallways, in a forgotten room behind a supply closet. When she turned the knob and found it unyielding, she realized that it had already been locked, to keep accidental snoopers from coming upon their secret meeting place where they drank smuggled-in wine and ate decadent food and discussed the most naughty novels ever published. She rapped on the door lightly and a few seconds later, coordinator Gabrielle Pope opened it a few inches, then smiled.

"Glad you could join us, Page."

Gabrielle opened the door wider. Page walked inside the dimly lit room that was furnished with an elegant table and plush chairs. Her glance fell on the other four members—Cassie Goodwin, Wendy Trainer, Jacqueline Mays and Carol Snow. They all greeted her warmly, and Wendy hurried to pour a glass of wine for Page.

"Cassie was just telling us about her experience seducing the man of her dreams," Wendy said in a sing-song voice.

Judging from Cassie's glow, her seduction had been successful, Page guessed, and she felt a rush of joy for the young woman she'd grown fond of. But Page's heart was beating like the wings of a hummingbird from her pent up anxiety. "I'm sorry, Cassie, I don't mean to interrupt, but please, I have to say something before I lose my nerve."

The women all looked surprised and their leader Gabrielle said, "Certainly. What's on your mind?"

Page took a deep drink from the glass of wine Wendy had given her, then swallowed hard and blurted, "The man of my dreams is my boss, Richard Armstrong. I'm going to seduce him with the lessons I learned in *Venus in Furs* by Leopold von Sacher-Masoch."

It was within the pages of *Venus in Furs* that she'd first begun to realize the power that a woman, even a mousy woman, could exert over a man in authority. She had imagined herself in Wanda's shoes a thousand times, wearing a decadent fur coat and wielding her feminine sway over her lover. The fantasy always left her feeling heady.

Page lifted her chin, then peered around the room warily, half afraid the women were going to burst out laughing at how high she'd set her sights.

Finally, Gabrielle broke the quiet with an approving noise. "Excellent choice. A story in which a woman so bewitches a man that he becomes subservient to her." The group coordinator looked pleased...and intrigued. "Have a seat, Page. After we hear from Cassie, we'll talk more about how you're going to show your boss... who's the boss."

2

FROM BENEATH HER LASHES, Page watched Richard pace as he dictated. He was so handsome when he was absorbed in thought. His long stride was even, almost melodic. His strong profile seemed even more serious, more masculine.

"I am in receipt of the signed non-disclosure agreement," he said.

Her hand moved automatically to record his words in shorthand. Her boss had worn his grey pin-stripe suit—her favorite. His jacket hung on a valet stand in the corner. His crisp white shirt contrasted nicely with his black hair that was slightly ruffled from jamming his hand through it.

He reached the south-facing window of his Buckhead office and paused to look at the Atlanta skyline. She sensed that he wanted to be out there, away from the office, which only made her admire him more for being so dedicated to the business. Richard had his own fortune—after his father's death he could've closed the company and lived a life of leisure, but was instead honoring his father's legacy and using the resources of Armstrong Enterprises to continue incubating worthwhile products that might not otherwise make it to market.

To her, he was heroic.

Richard turned away from the window to retrace his steps toward his desk. He seemed to struggle to pick up his train of thought. "Um…please review the enclosed prototypes and return the production bid sheet at your earliest convenience. Armstrong Enterprises looks forward to your response, et cetera, et cetera," Richard said, rolling his hand.

Page crossed her legs, hoping Richard would notice her new shoes, and her new dress—both on loan from Wendy Trainer since Page's budget couldn't withstand the full wardrobe makeover the members of the book club insisted she needed. But to her dismay, Richard seemed oblivious to her new outfit and indeed, her new look—her stylish haircut, her new makeup. Instead, he had moved back to the window to stare out. His six-foot-four-inch physique was framed to her from behind. He was such a big, beautiful man.

"That'll be all for now," he murmured over his shoulder.

She wet her lips. If Richard wasn't going to notice her, it was time to take control. She'd rehearsed positive thinking phrases over and over with the members of the Red Tote Book Club. She was good at her job and she would no longer be relegated to menial work. It was time Jessica learned that Page outranked her. And it was time Richard learned he needed her…in every way.

I can do this…I can do this…

Page took a deep breath. "Richard, shouldn't we request distribution routes the company can guarantee for an eighteen-month rollout of the product?"

He turned his head and squinted at her.

Panic fluttered in Page's chest—she'd overstepped her bounds. Which made her goal of seducing Richard seem downright ludicrous in comparison. Good grief, what had she been thinking? She scooted to the front of her chair, prepared to make a run for it.

RICHARD STARED AT his father's—no, *his* assistant. Page Sharpe had served his father well for over five years, which was why Richard had kept her on. But admittedly, he hadn't given her much credence, relegating her to background work. He realized now that he'd ignored her because he'd seen her as an extension of his father and it had been too painful to acknowledge her. Her presence as a third-wheel in the office only highlighted his father's absence. Slowly, her words sank in, sending a myriad of emotions pummeling through him.

Page dropped her gaze. "I'm sorry, sir. It's not my place to tell you your business."

In sudden clarity, Richard realized that Page, with her fiery long red hair and luminous green eyes, was quite pretty. In fact...she was beautiful. The yellow dress she wore outlined her lithe figure to perfection...and the woman had one fantastic set of bare, tanned legs ending in lethal black stiletto heels. Why hadn't he noticed them before? With a mental shake, he brought himself back to the moment.

"I'll go," Page said, pushing to her feet.

"No, you're right," he said, holding up his hand. "Of course we should ask about distribution routes. I don't know where my mind is." Lately he'd just felt so...scattered.

"You've been working so hard since your father died," she soothed. "I don't know how you do it."

Her kind words broke something loose inside him, something he'd been keeping dammed up. He knew he was spread dangerously thin, but work had to be done, else Armstrong Enterprises would come to a grinding halt, and he couldn't let that happen to his father's company.

But in this moment of weakness, Richard conceded that for once, he wished he didn't have to make all the decisions. He was starting to feel as if his entire life was immersed in the family business. Yesterday he'd glanced at the calendar and realized most of the year had evaporated while he'd been barricaded inside the four walls of this office.

He couldn't respond, could only beseech her with his eyes to…do what? Richard suddenly felt exhausted.

Moving with authority, she removed his suit jacket from the valet stand in the corner of his office, then held it out behind him. "Richard, go home."

He blinked. "I can't," he protested, gesturing to his cluttered desk. "I have to—"

"I'll sort through your inbox," she cut in. "I'll have everything lined up for you tomorrow morning. Meanwhile, *go home.*"

She shook his jacket in a "do as I say" motion. Page was so appealing, he couldn't refuse. He extended his arms and allowed her to ease the jacket over his shoulders. The light touch of her fingers warmed him even through the layers of fabric. A sense of being taken care of wrapped him like a cocoon. A feeling of calm settled over him.

"When you get home," she said, steering him toward the door, "turn off your phone, and go to bed."

He opened his mouth to offer an argument, but she put her finger to his lips.

"If you don't go, I'll drive you myself."

The shocking sensation of her touch sent lust rocketing through him. Richard sucked in a breath. Both of them were still as their gazes locked and the air sizzled. He blinked and when he opened his eyes, he saw Page in a completely different light.

He...*wanted* her. How was that possible?

A rap on his closed office door broke the intense moment. Page dropped her hand just as the door opened and Jessica appeared. The woman frowned at Page. "The phone is ringing off the hook out here."

Page frowned back. "Then you'd better answer it, hadn't you?"

Jessica's jaw dropped and she glanced at Richard, as if she expected him to take up for her. When he didn't, the blonde screwed up her mouth and left the office in a huff.

Page turned and smiled up at him. She had a dimple under her right cheek, and her eyes were bright. "You should get going, Richard. I'll reschedule your appointments and make sure no one interrupts you at home."

He was suddenly seized by the desire to be interrupted...by Page. "If something comes up you think I should know about, call me." His throat constricted. "I trust your judgment, Miss Sharpe."

Richard waited for her to correct him, to ask him to call her Page. But when it became clear she wasn't going to, that she enjoyed having the upper hand even if it was only in how they addressed each other, excitement infused his chest. She pointed toward the door, and ordered, "Go," in a tone that brooked no argument.

Curiously, blood rushed to his cock. Richard went…before Miss Sharpe could notice just how her take-charge attitude had affected him.

BY THE TIME RICHARD arrived at his home, his exhaustion had fled. Instead, he felt like running a marathon. He loosened his tie and undressed slowly, willing himself to relax and take the opportunity to catch up on his rest, as the comely Miss Sharpe had directed.

But just the thought of her marching him around, taking control, sent lust arrowing through his body. It felt good to turn things over to her, if only temporarily. He trusted her to take care of office matters in his absence…he trusted her to take care of *him*.

The thought sent his mind in wayward directions. He'd never really noticed the slip of a woman until today, but she was a vision. Even now he could see the clear bottle-green of her eyes as they flashed at him, the mandate in her voice that she knew what was best, and he should just do as she said. At this moment, he was pretty sure the woman could make him do anything she wanted.

His hand lowered to the front of his boxers to massage his hardening length. At the pace he'd been working for the past several months, there had been no time for dating, no time for women at all. He hadn't even stopped long enough to acknowledge how tightly he was wound for release, but the tingling in his balls told him he was long overdue.

He reclined on his bed, but instead of closing his

eyes to welcome sleep, he closed his eyes and instantly, the image of Page Sharpe was there, telling him that if he didn't leave the office to get some rest, she'd drive him home herself.

And then what? Tuck him into bed....

Richard stroked his erection as if she was standing there, telling him to pleasure himself, for his sake, so he could get some rest...and for extra incentive, she unbuttoned the front of the yellow dress, revealing the smooth globes of her breasts spilling over a black lacy bra...

He climaxed with a groan that bordered on pain because it had been so long and because the inducement had been so unexpected...and so vivid.

Richard cleaned himself up, then crawled under the sheets to rest at last, his body depleted. One thing was sure...he would never look at Miss Sharpe the same way again.

3

WHEN PAGE WALKED THROUGH the door of Armstrong Enterprises the next morning, she had a spring in her step. She felt...confident...powerful.

Jessica looked up from her desk and eyed Page's teal-colored skirt suit suspiciously. "I made coffee," the woman mumbled.

"Thanks," Page said, then walked over to the coffee station to pour herself a cup. "Is Richard in yet?"

"No. And I don't think it's very professional of you to call him by his first name."

Page raised her eyebrows. "I've heard you call him by his first name plenty of times."

"*I* am Richard's assistant," the woman said.

Page angled her head. "And yet, I'm the one he left in charge yesterday." She sipped the coffee, then winced. "This coffee is a little weak—you should make another batch before Richard gets in." She set the offending cup on Jessica's desk, then turned and walked into Richard's office, closing the door on the woman's noises of sputtering protest.

Page walked over to the window and opened the curtains, smiling at the panoramic view of downtown Atlanta, thinking of how Richard must see it. The Armstrongs had invested in so many start-up businesses and so many incubator products in Atlanta over the past forty years, she'd bet Richard owned a brick in almost every building on the horizon. He had much to be proud of. But having a hand in so many ventures meant he was expected to attend awards dinners, public hearings, and stockholder meetings, usually in the evenings and on weekends, and now there was only one of him to cover obligations that he and his father had once divided. No wonder Richard was exhausted.

"Good morning, Miss Sharpe." His voice boomed into her thoughts.

She turned and, at the sight of Richard in a flawless black suit, her heart skipped a beat. Dark smudges still shadowed his blue eyes, but he looked more rested than when he'd left yesterday. And the way he studied her head to toe with appreciation, it was as if he was seeing her for the first time.

"Good morning, Richard," she returned warmly, feeling herself expand under his gaze. "Were you able to get some rest?"

"It took me a while to…relax, but then I managed to fall asleep. You were right—I needed to get away from the office for a while."

She nodded demurely, but inside she was doing cartwheels.

He seemed to break eye contact reluctantly. When he turned toward his massive cherry wood desk, his eyes widened. "Wow…I can't remember the last time I could see the top of my desk."

Page walked over to show him the system she'd

used. "The files are organized by color-coded tabs, arranged by importance and time-sensitivity."

He moved to stand next to her. "So white is the lowest-priority and red would be the most...hot?"

Page's nerve endings sizzled as voltage leapt between them. "That's right," she murmured, drawing strength from the chemistry that had sprung up around them since she'd started asserting herself.

"It looks complicated," he teased. "I might need some tutoring."

The way he looked at her was almost...inviting. Page's pulse clicked higher when she realized that Richard was making himself accessible to her. In *Venus in Furs,* Severin had made himself available to Wanda in a similar fashion, testing the waters. A flush worked its way over her body. Maybe her idea of seducing her boss wasn't so far-flung after all.

It appeared he was...amenable.

A sharp rap at the door interrupted them. Page looked up to see Jessica walk in, carrying a cup of steaming coffee. The blonde smiled at Richard. "I thought you could use some fortification this morning. I made it strong the way you like it."

Page bit her tongue and averted her gaze.

"Thank you," he said as he took the mug. "Jessica, Miss Sharpe will be explaining her filing system to me and helping me get caught up today. Would you mind bringing her a cup of coffee, too?"

Jessica's smile turned stiff. As she turned she shot lasers at Page, but left the office and returned a few minutes later with two cups of coffee. She handed one to Page and kept one for herself, then she perched on the corner of his desk with familiarity. "What can I do to help?" she asked, gesturing to the neat stacks of files on his desk.

"See that Miss Sharpe and I aren't disturbed," he said bluntly.

Jessica straightened so quickly she sloshed her coffee. Page almost felt sorry for her—but not quite.

"Close the door, please," he added to the woman's retreating back.

When the door closed, it felt as if a vacuum had been created, sealing them in a cozy little chamber. His blue-eyed gaze latched on to Page and she couldn't look away. She tried to maintain a professional demeanor even though she was sure he could hear her heart pounding. But faking it had gotten her this far, so she simply picked up the cup of coffee for a sip and adopted her most authoritative voice. "Ready to get started?"

"Yes." Richard slipped off his suit jacket and hung it on the valet, then he turned back to her. "I'm in your hands."

When Page realized he wanted her to tell him what to do, a thrill ran through her. She pointed to his chair. "Sit."

He did, looking at her as if she was his teacher and at the neat stacks of folders as if they were shiny school supplies.

She reached for the folder on top of the stack marked with a red tab. As she reached past him his nostrils flared—inhaling her perfume? "Remember that the red tabs signify the high priority items."

"The hot items," he repeated.

"That's right." She opened the folder. "Top priority at the moment is tomorrow morning's meeting with

DPH Energy. James Dillingham and his team are bringing two prototypes of fuel cells for venture funding consideration." At any point in time, Armstrong Enterprises had a couple dozen products under review for venture funding. Richard had always handled the countless day-to-day support activities, but his father had always handled the initial product selection.

"I read all the collateral from DPH," Richard said. "But I haven't decided which prototype, if either, warrants funding."

"DPH sent more research," she said, holding up a folder.

His mouth tightened. "Dad was so good at cutting through the paperwork and the hype, as if he had some sort of second sense about the next big thing. I guess I just don't have the knack for it yet."

"Richard, you've done an amazing job handling everything since your father's passing."

He looked up at her, his expression troubled. "Do you really think so?"

Knowing that he cared about her opinion made her heart flower. "Yes, I do. But have you thought about hiring someone to relieve some of your workload?"

He nodded. "It's been in the back of my mind. I guess the thought of bringing someone else into that role feels like a betrayal to my father."

"I don't think your father would feel that way at all. Surely continuing to grow the company is the best homage you can pay to his legacy."

His anxious expression relaxed. "You're right. Of course, you're right, Miss Sharpe. Will you help me start the process of finding a candidate?"

"Of course. Why don't I take a stab at writing a job description, and we'll go from there?"

He looked relieved. "That would be excellent. Thanks."

It felt natural to reach down and squeeze his arm in reassurance. Beneath the crisp fabric of his shirt, his muscle bunched under her touch. The shock of the subtle response sent a pang of longing to her midsection. Richard's hands were large and broad, his fingers thick and blunt-tipped. What would it be like to have those fingers moving over her body...inside her body? Her fantasies ran rampant. With great effort, she forced her concentration back to the job at hand: proving to Richard that she deserved his trust and respect.

As the day progressed, two subtle changes occurred. Richard sat back and allowed Page to exert more and more control as they moved through the paperwork on his desk to complete the tasks on his substantial to-do list. And their body language began to mimic the role reversal of secretary bossing boss.

She stood over him as he returned phone calls and nodded approvingly. She leaned in to review notes and memos, their arms brushing. And later, when it became obvious that both of them craved more contact, she slid a complimentary hand over his shoulder or back as the "completed" stack grew taller. Richard's breath would hitch in his throat or a muscle would jump in his jaw. A couple of times he shifted in his chair and she wondered if under the desk he was sporting an erection.

They ordered lunch in. When Jessica delivered the bags, she shot Page a hateful look. By this time, Page and Richard were working in tandem, handing phones back and forth, arms crossing as files and memos were exchanged. When Jessica stuck her head in at five o'clock to say she was leaving, they barely looked up.

After they were alone, Richard loosened his tie and rolled up his shirtsleeves. Page removed her suit jacket to reveal a cream-colored sleeveless shell. Under his gaze, her nipples budded through the thin fabric. She knew he noticed because his hands flexed, then he jammed his fingers into his hair and looked away.

Knowing that she could affect him made her feel brazen…bold. If suddenly he was preoccupied, she was alert. In fact, the more distracted he became, the more focused she became. Finally, when she had to repeat a question, Richard sat back and pulled a hand down his face.

"I'm sorry, Miss Sharpe, I guess I still haven't caught up on my sleep."

She pushed to her feet. "Let's call it a night. You have the DPH meeting in the morning."

"Right." He shoved a stack of folders into his briefcase, then checked his watch and groaned. "I have to go by the Southern Entrepreneurs reception this evening."

"Actually, you don't," Page said. "I phoned the co-ordinator and made your excuses. I hope that was okay."

He pursed his mouth. "No, that's…great."

"Richard, you're trying to do too much," she warned. "You have to slow down."

A challenging light came into his eye. "And if I don't?"

She lifted her chin. "The future of this company is too important to risk. If you don't slow down, I'll tie you down to get some rest if I have to."

Page wanted the words back as soon as she'd said

them…what had she done? She had read the story of *Venus in Furs* so many times, she'd started believing that she could seduce her boss into becoming subservient to her. She stood still and waited for Richard to fire her for insubordination.

Richard looked a little dazed. Then he seemed to gather himself, leaned forward, and said, "Is that a promise, Miss Sharpe?"

4

WHEN RICHARD AWOKE, his body was rigid with need and Page Sharpe was on his mind. Her threat to tie him down had kept him awake half the night relieving his persistent hard-on, yet here he was with another erection. Before he could reach down and remedy the situation, his cell phone rang from the nightstand. Still groggy, he opened the phone and croaked, "Hello?"

"Richard?"

He blinked in shock to hear the voice of the woman he'd been dreaming about. "Miss Sharpe?"

"Is everything alright?"

"Except for the dream I had—" he began. When he swung his legs over the side of the bed and saw sunlight streaming through the tiny opening in the curtains, his heart leapt to his throat. "What time is it?"

"9:30 a.m."

He sprang to his meet. "The DPH Energy meeting was at nine."

"Yes, they're here. Are you okay? What was that about a dream?"

"Nothing," he said, massaging the bridge of his nose. "Can you stall for a few minutes?"

"I'll do my best."

Which meant, of course, that she would take care of everything capably and seamlessly, like always. His chest expanded with gratitude. "Thank you, Miss Sharpe."

"You're welcome, Richard."

He closed the phone and sprang into motion, taking a record-breaking shower and driving to the office as fast as traffic would allow. He slipped into the meeting forty minutes late, lifted his hand in apology to everyone, and slid into the nearest chair.

At the other end of the table, James Dillingham, head of DPH Energy, was describing the differences between the two fuel cell prototypes to Page, who was listening intently. When James paused, she asked two insightful questions that Richard admitted he couldn't have asked—the woman had done her research, while most of the information he'd read about the fuel cells remained a blur. In fact, he was having a hard time keeping up with the discussion.

Dillingham looked up. "Richard, do you have any questions?"

Richard tried to look confident instead of confused. "None."

The man smiled and rubbed his hands together. "Good. So when can we expect an answer?"

At a loss, Richard looked to Page. She, in turn, smiled at Dillingham. "Give us a couple of weeks to perform due diligence."

The man nodded and dismissed his team, who filed out of the meeting room. Then he walked to Richard and extended his hand.

"Sorry I missed the beginning of the presentation," Richard said.

"No problem," James said. "Page has a good handle on things, and I'm leaving photos and a demonstration DVD." He leaned in and lowered his voice. "You'd better take care of that one—I know a dozen executives who'd give their right arm for an assistant that smart... and that good-looking."

Richard followed the man's line of sight to Page, who was dressed in a chic avocado green suit with a short skirt and a short, swingy jacket. Her luscious red hair was swept up in some kind of knot that managed to be professional and sexy at the same time. Jealousy shot through Richard that James had been ogling her for the past hour. Page happened to look up and the impact of her poised smile was like a punch to the gut.

James clapped him on the shoulder. "Give me a call if you have any questions about the prototypes."

"Will do," Richard said, rankled.

Dillingham walked out, leaving him alone with Page. Richard walked up to her and crossed his arms in an effort not to touch her. "You were very impressive."

She dismissed his praise with a wave. "I asked the questions I thought you and your father might ask."

"Except neither my father nor I were here," he murmured. "I owe you for making us look so good."

"That's my job."

"I know," he said. "But let me take you to dinner this evening as thanks for all your hard work. You pick the place."

She pursed her mouth. "I'll think about it."

At her unwillingness, his cock stirred. An alien feeling invaded his chest: desperation. Why did it suddenly feel like his happiness hinged on Miss Sharpe saying yes?

PAGE WANTED TO SHOUT yes to Richard's invitation, but over the past couple of days, she'd sensed that he liked it when she was in control. So, just as Wanda had treated Severin in *Venus in Furs,* Page had kept Richard guessing for a while.

All day, in fact. Every time they passed in the hallway or she walked in front of his office, she felt his gaze tracking her. The knowledge that he wanted her tugged at her midsection, sending moisture to her thighs throughout the day.

After Jessica had left for the day, Page could feel Richard hovering. When she turned around, he was standing there looking for all the world like a teenage boy waiting to hear if she was going to accept his invitation to the prom.

"Have you decided, Miss Sharpe?"

"I've decided yes, Richard. I'll let you take me to dinner."

He looked relieved.

"But first I have to stop by my apartment to change—do you mind following me there?"

"Not at all," he said quickly.

On the drive to the apartment, Page perspired profusely. Maybe this was a bad idea…after all, Richard was still her boss…and there were laws against sexual harassment. She needed reassurance. While sitting at a red light, she called Red Tote Book Club member Wendy Trainer, the person who had been most instrumental in her outward makeover.

"Help!" Page said when Wendy answered. "My boss is following me back to my apartment."

"I thought that was the plan," Wendy said. "We went over it a dozen times."

"I'm having second thoughts," Page said. "I mean, this is my *job*."

"We discussed that, too. You don't really work directly for him, right?"

"Technically, I was his father's assistant, and when his father died, the son kept me on. But the point is, if things become too awkward, I'll be the one leaving, not him."

"If it comes to that, do you really think you'll have trouble finding another job?"

"No," Page admitted. "In fact, a client who was in this morning pulled me aside and gave me his card in case I was ever interested in a career change."

"There you go," Wendy said. "If the son turns out to be an ass about this, you can leave the company."

Page pressed her lips together.

"What?" Wendy asked. "What aren't you telling me?"

She winced. "That I've been in love with Richard for five years."

Wendy made a rueful noise. "Well, that does complicate matters, but you have to do what everyone else in the group is doing when it's their turn to seduce the man of their dreams—weigh the worst-case scenario against the best-case scenario."

"Worst-case scenario," Page murmured, "is that Richard will be appalled by my behavior, turn me down flat, and I have to leave the company because I can't face him."

"And we already established that you could get a job elsewhere. So…best-case scenario?"

Page sighed. "That it's everything I dreamed it would be."

"Ding, ding, ding! I think we have an answer. Have fun." Wendy hung up.

Page disconnected the call and smirked. Wendy was brash when it came to someone else's seduction…but how would the woman be when it was time for her own adventure?

The headlights of Richard's Mercedes in her rearview mirror was both comforting and terrifying as she pulled into the parking lot of her apartment building. Page parked, then got out and gestured for him to park, too.

"Come on up. I'll change, then we'll have a drink here before we go out."

Richard looked stiff and out of place as he climbed the stairs to her second floor apartment. Page was on the verge of hyperventilating, but she kept reminding herself that in the book that had so inspired her, Wanda also had been, at first, uncertain about assuming a dominant role over the man she cared about.

Page knew that part of the allure for Richard would be her pretending as if she knew what she was doing. So she marched with purpose and unlocked the door to her apartment even though she had to hold the key with both hands to keep it steady.

"Maybe I'd better wait in my car," Richard offered.

"Don't be silly," Page said over her shoulder. "It won't take me long to change."

"You look fine now…beautiful, even."

She turned and gave him a calm smile that belied her pounding heart. "I can do better than this."

His Adam's apple bobbed.

Page pushed open the door to her place and preceded him inside. Her apartment was small, but comfortable. She couldn't afford luxurious furnishings, so she'd made the most of sparse pieces with classic, clean lines. Richard nodded at her living room of creams and browns and grays with approval.

"Very nice."

"Thank you. I like it." She walked through the living room and pointed to a cabinet just inside the kitchen. "Would you mind helping yourself to the bar?"

"Not at all. What can I make for you?"

"A martini, please. And don't be stingy on the vodka," she ordered.

He gave her a little salute and headed in that direction, while Page veered off to the bedroom and closed the door. She leaned on the knob for support, breathing deeply to calm her galloping heart. The moment of truth was at hand, but in order for her to pull off the role reversal, she couldn't reveal to Richard how acutely she craved his touch. And if he did touch her, it would take all her acting skills to remain in control.

Page stared at the outfit borrowed from Wendy that she'd laid on her bed.

Could she go through with this?

5

RICHARD WANTED TO GULP his bourbon and Coke, but mindful of the drive to the restaurant, he sipped while waiting for Miss Sharpe to emerge from her bedroom.

Her *bedroom*.

What was he doing? He ran a finger around his shirt collar, wishing he could loosen it, but not daring to do anything to make himself more comfortable. He had no business standing here imagining her on the other side of the door undressing. He wasn't even sure what to make of this sudden attraction to a woman he'd known for years, but whom he'd never noticed.

To take his mind off his swelling cock, he glanced around the apartment, trying to get a sense of her life. Did she have a boyfriend? There was no indication that anyone lived with her, no masculine accessories. The only pictures were of an older red-haired woman who had the same green eyes as Page.

Page's television was tiny, her bookshelves over-loaded. He glanced at the titles, noting a range of interests from biographies to current novels to the classics, and remembered that she belonged to a book club. In a chair lay a red canvas tote, with a book peeking out. Curiosity to see what she was reading drove him to pull it out.

Venus in Furs by Leopold von Sacher-Masoch. Richard's pulse spiked. He didn't know the story, but he was familiar with the author—the man for whom the word *masochist* had been coined. Which meant the contents of the book had to do with sexual gratification through submission.

Feeling more feverish, he returned the book to the tote and took a hearty drink from his glass. He'd never in his life fantasized about being dominated by a woman—he'd always enjoyed being the aggressor in bed. But there was something so incredibly sexy about the idea of submitting to Miss Sharpe...maybe because it was so wholly unexpected. Regardless, the thought of her reading such naughty books made his cock throb. He had to get himself under control before she returned.

The bedroom door opened and he looked up.

And dropped his drink.

Page stood there dressed in a strapless black leather corset dress that outlined her full breasts and willowy figure to perfection, and killer platform stilettos six inches tall. The first thought that whipped through his mind was wondering how it would feel if she walked on his bare back.

She jammed her hands on her hips and nodded toward the broken glass at his feet. "You made a mess. Aren't you going to clean it up?"

The threatening tone in her voice sent a shudder of desire through him. "Of course." He scrambled to collect the broken glass, but clumsily managed to cut his palm in the process.

"Does it hurt?" she asked, walking over.

Richard nodded as pain shot up his arm. She led him to the kitchen where she held his hand under the faucet. When cold water hit the open gash, he sucked in a breath. "It stings."

"That's what you get for being careless," she murmured.

"I know," he said. "I'm sorry."

She turned off the water and pressed a towel against his hand until the bleeding stopped. "You might need stitches."

"No, I'm fine," he insisted. "But I dripped blood on your floor, on your shoes. I'm sorry."

She looked down at the drops of crimson oozing over the toes of her delicious shoes and *tsk, tsked.* "This is upsetting."

"I know. I'm sorry," he repeated, struggling to breathe. "Let me clean them for you."

Her mouth flattened as she considered his offer. She reached for the martini he'd made for her and took one deep drink, then another. Richard held his breath throughout. "Okay," she said finally. "You may clean them for me."

His cock surged.

She walked to a straight-back chair and sat down, then gave him an expectant look.

Richard moved slowly so he could memorize every detail. He knelt before her, heart pounding, then removed a handkerchief from his back pocket and used it to wipe the blood from the shiny surface of her shoes. Her legs were bare and lean, with the merest hint of tan. His breathing began to labor when he realized how badly he wanted to touch her...but he didn't dare without asking.

"You're beautiful," he whispered. "I love the dress."

"You don't think I put this dress on for you, do you?" she asked, eyebrows raised.

"No," he said quickly. "But I like it very much. And I want to touch you. I want to repay you for working so hard for me."

She angled her head. "You can touch me. But if this is truly repayment, then the touching should be one-sided."

He nodded. "Absolutely. I don't expect anything from you."

She gave him a little smile, then nodded, as if to say *proceed.*

Her permission sent relief and gratitude flooding his chest. He lifted her foot and removed the lethal-looking black stiletto. Her toenails were painted a deep red. He kissed the soft skin of her instep, and looked up to see the reaction on her face.

Her eyes were hooded with pleasure, her bare shoulders less rigid. Knowing that he was pleasing her made him even more excited. He continued to kiss her foot and ankle, working his way up to her knee before switching to the other foot and starting over. She made little breathy noises and scooted to the edge of the chair as he progressed upward. Her knees parted, revealing that she wasn't wearing underwear…and that she was a natural redhead.

Richard groaned and fell forward on her lap, trying to inhale her scent through the leather. When he lifted his head, he was eye level with her breasts straining at the lacings of the corset.

"Unlace my top," she ordered.

In his haste to obey, he fumbled with the thick ties,

but finally loosened the bindings and spread the top wide enough for her pink breasts to spill out. Her nipples were large and rose-colored. His mouth watered to suckle them, but he waited for her next command.

"Squeeze my nipples," she said.

He pinched the turgid skin between forefinger and thumb.

"Harder," she whispered.

He applied more pressure, pulling and rolling the tips until they were red and distended. "May I taste them?" he begged.

"No. Maybe some other time."

Put in his place, Richard kept fondling her nipples, conscious of his aching cock. She was killing him... and he loved it.

"Feel under my skirt," she directed.

Practically shaking, he pushed his hand between her knees until he encountered her wet, hot folds. He probed her, taking his cues from her expressions. "Miss Sharpe, tell me what feels good."

"Deeper," she insisted.

He pushed his fingers deeper inside her slick tunnel, imagining, wishing his body was engaged with hers. His thumb found the little nub of her center, but he was afraid to proceed.

"May I rub your clit?" he murmured.

"You could be more polite, Richard," she admonished.

"Please, may I rub your clit, Miss Sharpe?"

"Only with your tongue," she said.

At her erotic words, his cock oozed, begging for release. He withdrew his wet fingers, pushed up the leather skirt and shoved his face in the nest of auburn curls. He inhaled the heady scent of her, groaning. His cock ached in confinement. He pushed his tongue against her clit, then pulled it into his mouth. She tasted like the rarest delicacy, savory and sweet. He feasted on the morsel, increasing pressure in response to the sensual noises she made.

"Make me come, Richard," she ordered.

He stabbed at the button with his tongue until she began to tense. She drove her fingers into his hair and pulled his face harder against her secret place. He was drunk with the desire to please her. Her cries mounted, signaling her impending release. When she climaxed, the cream of her body bathed his tongue. He lapped it up greedily, happy to have anything of hers that she would give him.

When her contractions eased, she leaned back in the chair and lifted his head away from her. His mouth was wet and sticky from her, his cock rock hard behind his zipper. But from her warning that the touching would be one-sided, he knew his own release would have to wait until he was at home, in private. Knowing that his own pleasure would be postponed only ratcheted up his adrenaline.

Miss Sharpe sat back in the chair, still exposed to him, her red curls dark and wet from his mouth and her own lubricant, her breasts spilling over the corset. At the sated expression on her face, Richard felt more proud than he'd ever felt of any business accomplishment.

"Help me with my clothes so we can go to dinner," she said.

As directed, he pulled the corset closed over her breasts and carefully retied the lacings. The scent of her sex still

hung in the air like the most decadent perfume. He pulled
the skirt down to cover her treasure, then helped her to
her feet. He wanted her so much, he fairly trembled.

"You have my juices on your tongue," she said.
"Kiss me."

He kissed her but resisted the temptation to run his
hands up and down her body or push his stiff erection
against her. He was practically panting from the need
of her.

She pulled away first, then stepped back. "Now,
how about that dinner you promised me?"

When Page climbed in bed that night, she could
barely remember what she'd had to eat. Throughout the
meal, she'd had to pretend as if the encounter with
Richard hadn't been cataclysmic, pretend as if she
hadn't wanted to please him as much as he'd pleased
her. But it was all part of the plan to make him want
her even more...

She lay awake for hours, replaying the erotic scene
over and over until her entire body throbbed for his
touch. Some small part of her said that this situation
wouldn't last, couldn't end well.

But for now, she'd never felt so alive...

6

RICHARD HAD NEVER FELT so alive. One week, then another, passed in a pleasant, lust-filled haze. Every morning he raced to the office to see Miss Sharpe and follow her lead on to-do items for the day. And sometimes, if he was very lucky, she would allow him to come by her apartment after work and bring her to climax with his hands and mouth. She never touched him or allowed him to undress. He would drive home with a raging hard-on and barely make it inside before releasing his cock and pumping it to blessed gratification. But the satisfaction was always temporary.

He wanted Page. Wanted to sink into her as deeply as she could hold him and live between her thighs. Yet he conceded a great deal of satisfaction with the way things were—his days were much less stressful because Miss Sharpe guided everything with her able hand. He was sleeping well again, and he felt invigorated. He no longer thought about work every moment of the day.

Instead he thought about those amazingly sensitive nipples of hers that he hadn't yet been allowed to taste.

He heard footsteps and looked to the doorway of his office. His heart lifted to see Miss Sharpe standing there.

"I'm taking off," she announced.

"Okay," he said, as if there was anything else to say. She did what she wanted, when she wanted because she did it well.

"May I come over this evening?" He held his breath, hoping she would relent. He could almost taste her.

She considered him, then shook her head. "No, I don't think so. I have too much to do."

"Okay," he said, again powerless to argue. "Good night."

She turned and left without responding. He had to fight the urge to run after her, but he knew that would only irritate her. So he watched her until she disappeared from sight, his hands itching to touch her.

A few minutes later he heard a noise and looked up, hoping she'd changed her mind. Instead, it was only Jessica.

"Mr. Armstrong?"

He tried to hide his disappointment. "Yes?"

"James Dillingham is on the phone. He wants to talk to you about the fuel cell project."

"I've handed that project over to Miss Sharpe."

"He said it was important, sir."

Richard hesitated, not wanting to step on Page's toes, yet he didn't want to ignore Dillingham. "I'll take the call."

"Line two."

He punched the lighted button, then said, "Hello, James. What can I do for you?"

"I need to talk to you about the PEM fuel cell."

Richard's mind raced. "PEM?"

"Proton Exchange Membrane," James said, enunciating each word. "Remember, we classify the fuel cells by the type of electrolyte used to kick off the chemical reaction."

"Right," Richard said, although he was still fuzzy on the details. "What about it?"

"I called to correct some data on the reports before tomorrow morning's meeting. The efficiency for the PEM cell is actually coming in at around forty-five percent."

"Okay," Richard said carefully. "That's good... isn't it?"

Silence crackled over the line. "Good? That's ten percent off where it should be."

Richard winced at his gaffe.

A rueful noise sounded. "Richard, far be it for me to tell you your business, but lately...well, I'm a little worried about you, man. Maybe you should've taken some time off after you lost your dad. Everyone would've understood, you know."

Richard bristled. "James, just because I'm not up on every nuance of your technology doesn't mean I can't do my job."

James gave a little laugh. "Richard, that's precisely what it means. It seems to me that you've turned this project over to your secretary. The woman's smart and she has a great pair of legs, but a successful fuel cell could be the kind of product that puts a company in the position of going public. Don't you think it deserves your full attention?"

A sinking sensation settled in Richard's stomach. He shook his head, suddenly torn. How could he explain to the man that he liked it when Miss Sharpe was in charge? That it was exciting to see the woman he had thought was a little mouse come into her own sense of power. To see her in action, handling business and handling him, sent him to a level of sexual exhilaration he'd never felt before.

But James was right. It had been nice to temporarily offload his stress to someone who was willing to make decisions—it had been the perfect arrangement. He'd needed a break, and Miss Sharpe had been eager to have her contributions recognized. Their sexual chemistry had added another dimension to the situation—he fantasized constantly about her ordering him around in the bedroom, granting or denying him access to her body as she saw fit. She'd told him many times that she might never allow him to put his cock inside her. Even now, it made his body twitch with hope that she would someday change her mind.

At the realization of how much control over his life and body he had conceded to her, Richard closed his eyes. He was dismayed, shaken to the core, that he'd lost sight of his job, his mission, and his father's legacy. It was time to get back to business even though it would probably mean the end of his relationship with Page. The thought left him despondent, but he had a job to do, and a company to run. People were depending on him.

"Richard, are you still there?" James asked.

"Yes, I'm here," Richard said, feeling as if some kind of switch in him had been reset. "Could you have a complete copy of your report couriered to my house?" He gave the man the address, then ended the call.

He opened a desk drawer and removed a copy of *Venus in Furs*, the book that Miss Sharpe had been reading. He'd devoured it, fascinated by the story of Severin and Wanda, and how the man had shown his infatuation for her by becoming her slave. It helped him understand why he was driven to please Page, why he was willing to forego his own pleasure to heighten hers. The deprivation had, in turn, increased his own pleasure.

Richard nursed a pang for the phase that had just passed. For a staid businessman whose life was all about the family business, it had been exciting to live out a fantasy, even for a short time.

He hated to let it go…but it was time to get back to reality…

7

PAGE ARRIVED AT THE OFFICE the next morning feeling antsy and torn. She was enjoying her new responsibilities at work and was looking forward to the meeting with James Dillingham. But the game she was playing with Richard was starting to wear on her. In *Venus in Furs*, Wanda had begun to wish that Severin, the man who had offered himself up as her love slave, would be more aggressive in his life and in the bedroom. Page conceded that she was starting to have the same feelings about Richard. Because while it was heady to be able to command Richard to please her, she realized that she missed the old Richard, when he was decisive and take-charge.

She hurried into the office and found something disarming—Jessica, seemingly back to superior herself, considering the smirk on her face.

"Good morning," Page ventured, heading to the coffee pot. "Is Richard in?"

"Yes, and the DPH meeting is underway."

Page frowned and glanced at her watch. "It's not scheduled for another half hour."

"Richard changed his mind, asked James Dillingham to come in early."

Surprise and something near panic spiked in Page's chest. Was Richard trying to exclude her from the meeting?

She hurried toward the meeting room and rapped lightly before opening the door and sliding inside. Heads turned in her direction. She nodded to James Dillingham, then made eye contact with Richard. He looked spectacular in a navy blue suit, cream-colored shirt and lime green tie. His black hair was newly cut, giving him a boyish look. But there was nothing boyish about the set of his broad shoulders or the line of his jaw. Something—regret?—flickered in his blue eyes before he looked back to Dillingham and resumed the meeting.

Stung, Page claimed a seat at the end of the table. Something had changed—Richard was different. Back to the old Richard, confident and focused. She gathered from the conversation that he hadn't yet revealed to Dillingham that Armstrong Enterprises would be funding the PEM fuel cell. He must be keeping him in suspense and although she was feeling shut out of this final meeting, Page was glad she would at least be present for the announcement because she felt so invested in the project.

"So after careful consideration," Richard said, "I'm happy to announce that Armstrong Enterprises has chosen one of the two fuel cells produced by DPH Energy to fund. Armstrong will throw its influence—and money—behind the alkali fuel cell."

Amidst the cheers and back-slapping, Page's jaw dropped. The alkali version over the PEM version? She came halfway up out of her seat. "Richard, can we have a moment?"

He hesitated, then nodded and excused himself. She went out into the hallway and waited for him to close the door to the meeting room.

"What was that?" she asked. "I thought we discussed that the PEM version was superior to the alkali version."

A muscle worked in Richard's jaw. "That was your opinion. As it turns out, the efficiency of the PEM model is lower than expected."

She crossed her arms. "But the platinum electrode catalysts are pricey. And they can leak, which would be an environmental hazard."

A muscle worked in his jaw. "I understand your argument, Page, but I've made my decision."

She realized he was back to calling her by her first name...subtly exerting his rank over her...relegating her back to the role of his assistant. She shrank inside as waves of embarrassment over her recent behavior crashed over her.

Richard's expression was cold...professional. "I think I was under more stress than I realized since my father's death and allowed myself to be distracted these past couple of weeks from things that really matter. But I'm over that now."

Over *her,* she realized. She'd fallen more in love with him, and now he was repulsed by her. Her cheeks burned and she wanted to disappear. "I understand," she managed to say. "Perhaps it's best if I don't rejoin the meeting."

His mouth tightened. "I'm sure there are plenty of other things around here that need to be done."

She swallowed hard and inclined her head. With her heart breaking, she turned on her heel and walked back to the area she shared with Jessica.

"How was the meeting?" Jessica asked with a snarky smile. She had obviously picked up on the fact that Richard had re-established his position in the firm.

Ignoring the woman, Page reached into her briefcase and withdrew a folder. Inside was the job description she'd told Richard she would write as a first step to bringing in someone to take over the role his father had provided to the firm.

Venture capital firm seeking Acquisitions Director to scout products for funding and development. No minimum education requirements, but knowledge in many disciplines a necessity. Good research skills, financial and technical experience also required. Some travel, extra languages a plus. The ideal candidate is collaborative and willing to adapt and put in the hours necessary to escort a product to the marketplace. Must be able to work with no supervision, and should be passionate about their work.

Page bit her lip. Perhaps that last sentence was too much, but the job description she'd written for the person to replace Richard's father described the type of person Richard's father had been. It would take someone special to fill his shoes.

Her eyes watered. Too bad she wouldn't be here to meet that person. She had to leave, because she couldn't bear the way Richard had looked at her just now...couldn't endure working side by side with him, remembering the erotic experiences they'd once shared. He knew every inch of her body, inside and out, which strangely, now gave him the upper hand. Richard was obviously ashamed of their role-playing. But even if he never mentioned it again, it would always be in the room with them, overshadowing every exchange.

Page pulled out a piece of paper and scribbled a message on it, then attached it to the job description and sealed it in an envelope. "Can you make sure that Richard gets this?" she asked Jessica.

The blonde gave her a haughty look.

Page sighed. "Please?"

The woman held out her hand.

Page gave her the envelope and marched out, leaving Armstrong Enterprises and Richard Armstrong behind.

She certainly hoped that James Dillingham had been serious about offering her a job because she'd be needing one. Page blinked back tears as she unlocked and swung into her car.

Her seduction story for the Red Tote Book Club wouldn't have a happy ending after all.

8

PAGE WAS CURLED UP on her couch, drinking a glass of wine and trying to read a contemporary novel. But her mind raced in figure-eights and nothing seemed as appealing at the moment as re-reading her favorite classic, *Venus in Furs*. Finally she succumbed, reaching into the red canvas tote bag to withdraw the book. After many readings, the spine was broken and she'd dog-eared the pages of some of her favorite scenes.

She turned to the ending to read about the sad fate of Wanda, how she'd loved Severin enough to indulge in his fantasies, only to realize in the end that acting out the fantasies had, in fact, ruined their chance for love.

Page laid her head back on a cushion and allowed the tears to come. What Richard must think of her and her wantonness. Sure, he'd participated in their role-reversal game and had seemed to enjoy it, but apparently he'd gotten to the point where he was disgusted by their behavior.

She lifted her head to take a deep drink from her wineglass. Whatever. No matter how Richard felt about what they'd done, she refused to be ashamed anymore. They were single, consenting adults and during the course of their sex play, they hadn't hurt each other.

Well, except for the part where her heart had gotten broken.

Despite his rebuff, she couldn't stop thinking about their evenings together, and the way he had reveled in pleasing her. If she closed her eyes, she could feel his hands and mouth on her body now, bringing her to the heights of arousal. She might have seemed in command during their sessions, but little did Richard know, he had total control. If he had insisted on making love to her, she would have given him full access to her body, any time.

Her phone rang, breaking into her thoughts. She glanced at the caller ID and smiled a bittersweet smile when she saw Wendy Trainer's name. Page connected the call.

"Hello?"

"I got your text message," Wendy said. "What happened?"

"I don't know," Page said. "I guess he just changed his mind. He made it clear to me this morning that he was no longer interested in playing our little game. And he shut me out of an important meeting at work."

"What did you say?"

"I didn't say anything. I wrote a letter of resignation, then I left."

"And you haven't heard from him?"

Page blinked back fresh tears. "No."

A long sigh sounded over the line. "I'm sorry, Page. But you knew it could end this way. Do you have any regrets?"

"Just that it ended. But deep down I knew it couldn't last forever."

"What are you going to do now?"

The sound of the door bell ringing saved her from answering. Page pushed to her feet. "Hang on— someone's at the door."

"Omigod, is it him?" Wendy asked, her voice shrill with excitement.

Page's pulse tripped at the possibility, but she wouldn't let herself hope. She put one eye to the peephole. At the sight of Richard looking back, she gripped the phone tighter. "Yes, it's him. What should I say?"

"Seems to me that since he came to see you, he's the one who has something to say," Wendy offered. "Good luck."

Page ended the call and tried to calm her racing heart while she set down the phone and glanced in the mirror. She was still wearing the skirt and blouse she'd worn to work, sans the jacket and the heels. Fuzzy house shoes adorned her feet. Her once-neat chignon was now a loose knot, with as much hair falling down as was confined, but there was nothing to be done about it. She took a deep breath and opened the door.

Richard straightened and pinned her with his blue-eyed gaze. The mere sight of him in rolled-up shirt-sleeves and loosened tie was an assault on her senses.

"May I come in, Page?" Although he was asking permission, there was nothing in his demeanor that hinted of submission. And the fact that he was using her first name let her know he was boss.

She stepped aside and allowed him to enter. Curiously, he was carrying a large shopping bag from an upscale department store. He set it down with no explanation. A parting gift, perhaps?

Page closed the door behind him and crossed her arms to control her trembling. "Why are you here?"

"To try to talk you into coming back to work for me."

So he needed her at the office, not in his life. The tiny part of her that had hoped he'd come for a different reason disintegrated. "Surely you understand, Richard, that I can't be your assistant anymore."

He nodded. "I understand. That's why I was hoping you'd agree to be the Acquisitions Director for Armstrong Enterprises."

As his words sunk in, her mouth opened in astonishment. "You want me to take over your father's position?"

"I can't think of a better person, or anyone who's more qualified. You know how Dad worked, but you have your own mind. You're a passionate person." He reached forward to pick up her hand. "And I trust you."

She swallowed hard as his fingers burned into hers. "But you went against my recommendation with DPH Energy."

"Only because I had information you didn't have. That won't happen again."

Her vital signs were going haywire. "Are you sure we can work together after...everything that's happened between us?"

"It might be tricky," he admitted, pulling her closer. "There will have to be some rules." He lowered a smoldering kiss on her neck.

Page sighed as her entire body came alive. "What kind of rules?"

He lifted his head and looked into her eyes. "How

about I be the boss in the boardroom…and you be the boss in the bedroom?"

White-hot lust whipped through her body and a smile curved her mouth. "I like those rules."

He looked relieved. "May I kiss you, Miss Sharpe?"

"Only if you do it well," she returned.

He did. After a thorough laving of her mouth, he pulled back. "May I undress you?"

A shiver skated over her shoulders. "You may."

He began peeling off her clothes, one item at a time, until she stood nude before him.

He devoured her with his eyes. "You're so beautiful, Miss Sharpe. May I give you a gift?"

Surprised, she nodded.

He reached for the shopping bag and withdrew a large box. He handled it carefully, as if the contents were precious. Then he lifted the lid and withdrew a long black fur coat.

"It's the best synthetic fur money can buy," he offered.

Page smiled at the thought that Richard knew she would appreciate that no animals had been harmed for the coat. "For me?"

"Venus in furs," he murmured, then moved behind her and held out the coat.

"You know the book?" she asked, incredulous as he slid the luxurious coat onto her shoulders. The silky weight of it was heavenly…surreal.

"I snooped. And I can't think of anything more sexy than you wrapped in fur." He turned her around and looked her up and down, his smoky eyes hooded. "Miss Sharpe, may I make love to you?"

Happiness flowered in her chest even as her body

began to ready itself for him, warming and loosening and lubricating. She put her mouth to his ear. "Only if you do it well."

He removed his clothes in record fashion. When he stood nude before her, she was in awe of his male beauty and practically trembling from wanting him. His shoulders were thick, his thighs powerful, his erection imposing...and all hers.

He led her to the couch and guided her down. In the cloak of the sleek fur coat, she received his body in one massive thrust. It was a fullness she'd never known, both physically and emotionally. Their groans mingled as they acclimated to each other and fell into a sensual rhythm. She arched her back, meeting him in every stroke, sliding on the sumptuous furs.

"Make this last," she whispered, not wanting the erotic experience to end.

But as her own climax came on fast and furious, Page clutched at Richard's back. "I changed my mind—come with me...*now.*"

And he did.

A NEW CHAPTER

1

WENDY TRAINER LOVED BEING the center of attention...
usually. Being one of Atlanta's most successful party
planners required that she always be on her game, and be
quick on her feet. But at the moment she was sitting in
the hot seat at a meeting of the Red Tote Book Club.

She and four other women gathered monthly at a
branch of the Atlanta Public Library in a forgotten
room. To all outward appearances, it looked like any
other book club, but little did outsiders know, instead
of discussing books about shoe shopping and personal
melodrama, the women discussed some of the most
famous erotica novels ever written.

Under the guidance of their leader, Gabrielle Pope,
Wendy and the rest of the group were learning about
the evolving sexual roles of women, and how fantasies
and sex play could level the playing field between
lovers. Two months ago, Gabrielle had challenged the
members—Wendy, Cassie Goodwin, Page Sharpe, Jacqueline Mays and Carol Snow—to take their book discussion outside the low-lit room in which they met, and
use the lessons between the pages to seduce the man
of their dreams. Two members had reported success in
their missions, and Wendy was up next.

It was a lot of pressure.

"Wendy, do you have a man in mind for your seduction?" Gabrielle asked.

She bit her lip with trepidation, but finally nodded. "My best friend, Nate."

All around the table, eyebrows shot up.

"You want to seduce your best friend?" Page Sharpe asked.

The woman's green eyes glowed with an inner light of love found. Wendy wished her own baby blues would soon reflect such good fortune, but she had her doubts.

"I realize I've been in love with Nate most of my life," Wendy admitted. "He's…he's everything I've ever wanted in a man."

"Have the two of you ever dated?" Cassie asked.

"No." Wendy smiled. "Nate is literally the boy next door. We were in strollers together, learned how to ride bikes together. We went to the same school." She shrugged. "When we were at the age when we might have dated, I knew Nate had a crush on me, but I went for older guys, the bad boys. Nate was just my geeky friend, someone I'd known all my life."

"And when did that change?" Jacqueline pressed.

Wendy smiled in fond recollection. "About a year ago. I had planned a big birthday party for the ten-year-old son of an important client. I was told in no uncertain terms that the entertainment had to top anything that any of this kid's friends had had at their parties."

The women nodded in understanding.

"The boy was nuts about baseball, so I'd planned for the party favors to be official Braves jerseys, and for a batting cage to be delivered to the backyard. But at the last minute, the cage fell through. All the guests had arrived, and there was nothing for them to do. The party was shaping up to be a big dud, and I knew the client would blacklist me among her friends."

Wendy hugged herself. "I called Nate in a full panic. He told me to stall and he'd think of something. A few minutes later he shows up with one of the Atlanta Braves players, who is a client with Nate's law firm. The guy played catch with the birthday boy and signed everyone's jersey—the kids loved it." She sighed. "It's so like Nate to save the day. I watched him running around, playing with the kids, and this feeling just came over me. I realized I was in love with him."

"Did you tell him?" Gabrielle asked.

Wendy shook her head. "He was seeing someone at the time. But that ended a couple of months ago, and I've been trying to work up my nerve since then to tell him how I feel."

"What's stopping you?" Carol asked. Of all the women, she seemed to be the most skeptical about the group's exercise of seduction by the book.

A flush worked its way up Wendy's neck. "I don't have the best track record where relationships are concerned. Nate, on the other hand, isn't the kind of guy who has flings. He's gorgeous, but he's wired for fidelity and commitment." She stopped and glanced all around. "I'm afraid he'll laugh at me if I tell him I want a serious relationship with him."

"You're afraid he won't believe you?" Gabrielle asked.

"Right."

"So you've stayed in touch?"

"He still lives next door," Wendy said. "Both of our

parents retired and moved to Florida. Nate bought his parents' home and I'm renting from my parents. But while we see each other coming and going, we aren't really that close anymore. Sometimes I think Nate avoids me."

"But proximity helps," their leader acknowledged. "You need a plan. Is there a book we've read you think might help you?"

Wendy nodded. "*Fanny Hill* by John Cleland. Advice from one party girl to another, so to speak." Her cheeks warmed. "Fanny started out with a bit of a reputation, but eventually earned respect. That's what I'm hoping for in Nate's eyes."

The other women chorused their support for her chosen title. *Fanny Hill* had been one of the most fun books they'd read. The fact that the novel had been the source of moral outrage as recently as the 1960s was almost laughable because while Fanny's exploits had been naughty for a single woman of her era, the text itself was tame by contemporary standards.

"But I don't know what to do first," Wendy admitted. "How can I convince Nate that I'm ready for a serious relationship with him?"

Seemingly stumped, the women all sipped from their wineglasses and pulled on their chins.

Suddenly Jacqueline leaned forward. "What if you tell him you're ready for a serious relationship with someone else?"

Cassie nodded. "Good idea. If he thinks you're ready to change your ways for someone else, he might decide to throw his hat in the ring."

"Is he jealous where you're concerned?" Page asked.

Wendy pursed her mouth. "Maybe. He always stops me if I mention someone I'm dating—he said he doesn't want to hear about my 'men.'"

"Good," Gabrielle said, nodding. "If your Nate is willing to go out of his way to help you out of a jam, then tell him you've met someone you want to get serious with, and convince him you need his support to mend your partying ways."

"You mean, enlist Nate's help in his own seduction?" A grin bloomed over Wendy's face. "I like it."

2

NATE BERTRAM CHECKED HIS WATCH as he walked into
the midtown restaurant where he was supposed to
meet his best friend Wendy for lunch. He was right
on time but Wendy would be her requisite ten
minutes late, so he'd have time to make a couple of
phone calls.

They'd joked about meeting out in public when they
lived next door to each other, but lately he'd gotten the
feeling that Wendy was avoiding him at home, so a
neutral meeting place to talk had seemed appropriate.
He quieted the nagging voice in his head that something was wrong…that something between him and
Wendy had changed…

Nate sighed. He hoped he hadn't made a mistake by
asking Wendy to coordinate a retirement party for one
of the partners at his law firm. He needed it to be a
stately affair, and stately wasn't the word that Wendy
Trainer conjured up.

Vivacious. Leggy. Sexy.

But not stately.

She would come cartwheeling into the restaurant
wearing a skimpy outfit that defied the laws of science,
turning every head. Men worshipped her, women tol-

erated her. Wendy was rarely the most gorgeous girl in the room, but her big, sunny personality made her irresistible.

He should know. He'd been trying to resist her his entire life.

Pushing down an all-too-familiar sense of frustration, Nate walked to the hostess station to request a table for two for Bertram.

"Your party is already seated," the woman said, then led him into the dining room.

Nate blinked in surprise. The only time Wendy had ever been early for anything was if she hadn't yet gone home the night before.

When he spotted her checking her BlackBerry, he did another double-take. Since when did the woman who owned the record for slamming tequila shots at the Honeysuckle Bar own a black pin-stripe pant suit? And he wouldn't have thought it possible to tame her wild blond curls into a chignon.

"Who died?" he said, sliding into the chair opposite her.

Wendy looked up and grinned. Even without the blue eye shadow and bright pink lipstick, her smiling face would not be repressed. "Hey, you." Then she pouted. "You don't like my new look?"

To hide his physical reaction to the prim but snug outfit, he unfolded the napkin at his plate and draped it over his lap. "It's a nice suit. I just didn't think you owned such an animal."

She arched an eyebrow. "Just because you've known me since the sandbox, Nate, doesn't mean you know everything about me."

He took a drink from his water glass. She had that right. He knew that Wendy preferred cherry popsicles over strawberry, and that she had an irrational fear of snails, but he'd never heard her sigh after a deep, thorough kiss. Holding their noses to kiss when they were nine didn't count.

Wendy put her shoulders back and pulled on the lapel of her jacket. "I'm trying to get into the mood to arrange this somber retirement party for your partner."

"I didn't say 'somber,' just—"

"Boring?" she cut in.

"Dignified," he corrected. "Think you can handle that?"

"I'm on it," she said, pushing a folder across the table. "I came up with a list of locations and menu suggestions, plus a couple of designs for invitations, all very classy." She smiled. "Let me know what you think when you've had a chance to read over them."

Impressed, he nodded. "Will do."

They ordered food, then Nate sat back in his chair. "So...what's new besides the wardrobe and the hair?"

Wendy tugged on her ear—a telltale sign that something was up...something she didn't want to share.

"Spill it," he admonished. "This is me, remember?"

She nodded and smiled, then clasped her hands together on the table. "Promise you won't laugh?"

"Absolutely not," he said with grin.

But she didn't return the smile. "I mean it, Nate."

He sobered and sat forward. "Okay. What's up?"

She worried her lower lip with her teeth for long, agonizing seconds during which all kinds of catastrophes rolled through his mind. She was broke. She was moving. She was sick. At last, she lifted her blue-eyed gaze. "I met someone."

He relaxed back into his chair. "Is that all?"

"Nate...I think it's serious."

His stomach knotted. He'd never heard Wendy used the "s" word before. "Okay," he said carefully. "So who is this guy?"

She gave a dismissive wave. "You don't know him."

That was good at least. He was tired of having to pull away from friends simply because he couldn't bear to hear them talk about how amazing Wendy was in bed. "So what's with the long face?"

"I need your help," she said.

Nate spread his hands. "With what?"

She seemed to be struggling for words. "The thing is...this guy reminds me a little of you. And I have to change my image, if I intend to keep him. I have to convince him that I can settle down."

Reminded her of him? It hurt knowing she wanted a facsimile when she could have the real him. "I don't see where I come in."

She reached forward to clasp his hand. "I need for you to help me understand how this guy thinks, the things he might like and the things I need to avoid doing."

Nate frowned. "Wendy, you shouldn't change for anyone. If the guy doesn't like you for who you are, he's not the one for you."

"But he is the guy for me," she said. "I love him, Nate."

His throat convulsed painfully. Throughout Wendy's many, many relationships during high school, college and since, he'd never seen her like this. It took his breath away because he'd always hoped that if she ever had that look in her eye, it would be for him.

She squeezed his hand. "It's important I don't mess this up. Will you help me, Nate?"

He glanced down at her soft, slender fingers and conceded this was the only kind of caress he would ever receive from Wendy. He lifted his gaze to hers and swallowed the words he really wanted to say in favor of, "Of course. What can I do?"

3

WENDY PEEKED OUT THE WINDOW of her second-floor bedroom, down onto the backyard of the house next door where Nate was mowing the lawn. Typical for an Atlanta summer, the sun blazed down. His dark hair was spiked with perspiration. He stopped often to remove a bandanna from the back pocket of his faded work jeans and wipe his brow.

Watching Nate mow the lawn was one of her favorite pastimes. He always looked so deep in thought, his handsome profile set in concentration as he deftly maneuvered around the base of the massive oak tree they'd climbed when they were children and where they'd carved their initials.

He stopped and leaned over to toss a rock out of the path of the mower. When he straightened, he lifted the hem of his sweat-soaked T-shirt and peeled it off.

Wendy's mouth went dry. Somewhere between tenth and twelfth grade, Nate had started bulking up. During college, his arms and shoulders had continued to thicken, and now, as a full-grown man, he was packing some serious muscle. His broad chest tapered into a narrow waist and washboard abs covered with just enough hair for a woman to run her fingers through. His skin was baked to a fine golden brown from outdoor work and weekend softball.

He was sexy as hell, she conceded. His former girl-friend, Susan or Suzanne or whatever, had been crazy to let him go and move to Boston.

Wendy sighed. Of course, what did it say that the sexiest man alive had been under her own nose all this time and she'd been oblivious?

Nate turned the mower around to make another pass, staring over the fence at the amazing Grecian key design cut into her own backyard. When she'd hired the college-aged son of a client of hers to mow the grass during the day while Nate was working, she hadn't counted on the fact that the kid was a budding graphic artist.

Nate glanced up in the direction of her bedroom window. Wendy jerked back, self-conscious about spying on him. After all, she was supposed to be crazy about some other guy…a guy she realized she needed to invent a backstory for in case Nate asked.

She peeked out the window as he turned and headed away from her. The sun glistened off the perspiration on his muscled back. Her fingers itched to touch the smooth, corded skin. He was so sexy, she could eat him up. As longing welled in her midsection, her hand slipped into the waistband of her shorts.

Lately her fantasies had centered exclusively around Nate doing amazing things to her with the mouth that had whispered the password to their tree house, with the fingers that had taught her how to tie her shoes, with the body that had slid home in countless little league games where she'd cheered him on from the dugout.

Her fingers sneaked into the nest of fine hair between

her thighs until she found her pleasure treasure. Then she worked the little nub like she imagined Nate would if only he'd realize how perfect they would be together.

People—Nate included—assumed because she'd dated a lot of guys, she must have had lots of great sex…but that simply wasn't the case.

Quantity did not equate to quality.

With every guy, there was something missing. Her body would be engaged, but not her mind. Lately, more times than not, she would replace the face of the man angled above her in bed with Nate's…and afterward, she'd be left with a profound sense of disappointment that it hadn't been him.

She knew every inch of his face, the way a faint dimple appeared under his left cheek when he smiled, the way his brow furrowed under duress. She imagined that intense expression of concentration focused on her, on her body, delivering the deep satisfaction that only someone who cared about her could deliver. If she could persuade Nate to come to her bed, she was sure he would memorize her secret places just like he'd memorized her favorite color of peony pink and her favorite vegetable combination of mashed potatoes and peas.

Yes, if Nate was pleasuring her, she told herself as her fingers danced over the sensitive nub, he would be using his tongue, the same tongue he'd used to seal the envelope that held the official rules of the Secret Society of the Nate and Wendy Clubhouse.

She stroked her folds, now slick with moisture, faster and harder, until the disturbance in her womb erupted into a full-fledged storm that swept in ever-tightening circles until it converged into one explosive eye. Her knees buckled and she cried out Nate's name, again and again. Her body pulsed with latent spasms and as she recovered, she marveled that if the mere thought of him making love to her could trigger that kind of response, what earth-shaking reaction might he be able to elicit from her body if he were actually in the same room with her?

The whir of the lawn mower ended abruptly. Wendy pulled herself together and ran downstairs, taking them two at a time. At the bottom of the stairs, she turned and jogged through the hallway into the kitchen, picked up a half-full bag of garbage and bounded out the back door.

Nate paused from pushing the mower back to his garage and waited for her to catch up on the other side of the fence. "Hey. I didn't know if you were home."

"I'm home," she said, lifting the lid on the garbage can to drop the bag inside. She stuffed her hands into the pockets of her shorts to keep from reaching out to drag her fingers across his sweaty chest.

"I was going to mow your grass," he said, then nodded. "But I see you beat me to it."

"Oh, that. My boyfriend stopped by and mowed it."

His eyebrows arched. "Is he a landscape designer?"

Wendy wet her lips. It sounded as good as anything she could make up. "As a matter of fact, he is."

The corners of his mouth quirked. "Well, he cuts a mean yard."

Wendy frowned, realizing that a brain surgeon or a stock broker might've made Nate more jealous. "He owns his own landscaping company," she offered as supplemental material.

"Good for him," Nate said, running the T-shirt over

his hard, glistening body. "What's this guy's name and when do I get to meet him?"

Wendy tore her gaze from Nate's abs. "His name is…Dalton." A city north of Atlanta, but it would work. Then she angled her head. "You've never wanted to meet any of my boyfriends."

Nate pursed his mouth. "True. But this guy is more than a boyfriend, right? If I'm going to help you close the deal, don't you think I should meet him?"

"He…travels a lot for his job," she said, making up the story as she went along.

Nate squinted. "For landscaping?"

"He has…a far-reaching clientele."

"Is Dalton his first name or his last name?"

"Um…his first name," she said. "Nate, did you get a chance to look over the information for your coworker's party?"

"Not yet," he admitted. "But I'll read it tonight and call you later."

She made a rueful noise. "I'm going out…with Dalton. Can we meet for lunch tomorrow? Near Lenox?"

He nodded. "Okay. See you then."

Wendy turned to walk back toward her house. When Nate was out of earshot, she smiled to herself and murmured, "You'll see a lot more of me tomorrow than you think."

4

"THE CAFÉ IS THIS WAY," Nate said, pointing to the right inside the entrance to the massive structure known as Lenox Mall.

Wendy turned back. She wore a plain navy dress that looked great on her despite the fact that it covered twice as much skin as she normally bared. Nate suddenly realized how much he missed her cleavage. No surprise, considering he'd been looking at it ever since Wendy had announced when they were eleven that she was wearing an alien contraption known as a training bra.

"I know," she said. "But I was hoping we could take a little side trip." Her eyes turned pleading. "I need to buy a few things, and I'd like your opinion."

A sour taste settled in his mouth. "For Dalton?"

She nodded. "Please, oh, please, Nate?"

He frowned, irritated with himself that he'd spent most of the previous evening looking out the window, hoping to get a glimpse of the wonderful Dalton when he came to pick her up for dinner, yet had somehow missed the guy. "What kinds of things?"

"You'll see," she said, grasping his hand and pulling him along.

Just like the time she'd dragged him to the dunking

tank at the county fair, Nate recalled. She'd somehow talked him into volunteering to sit on the platform and taunt the bullies trying to hit the bull's-eye. Within five minutes, he'd gone swimming.

He got the same feeling of having the platform fall out from under him when Wendy veered toward an upscale lingerie store.

Nate stopped dead in his tracks, staring at the scantily clad mannequins in the window. "What's this?"

She scoffed. "It's lingerie, silly."

He pushed out his cheek with his tongue. "I can see that. What are we doing here?"

Her blue eyes were wide and innocent. "You said you'd help me pick out some things."

Blood rushed away from Nate's brain to more urgent areas…it was the only way he could explain the plan that was formulating in his head. Wendy wanted him to help her pick out lingerie. The fact that it was for another man was secondary. When would he get another chance like this? He could watch her sort through and fondle lacy unmentionables *with her permission.*

He made a rueful noise. "Okay."

Her panoramic smile alone was reward enough, but he'd underestimated the impact of standing next to her while surrounded by sexy bras and panties and skimpy sleepwear. As she walked from station to station, touching, peering, studying, Nate's mouth watered as if he were in a bakery. Indeed, the way the store was merchandised, by color and in tiered racks, it looked like a candy store.

"What do you think?" she asked, holding up something that resembled a red satin slingshot.

"What is it?"

"A thong." And then as if he needed a demonstration, she held it over her stomach. "They're panties with no backs," she said, flipping them around to show him the tiny red ribbon that apparently was supposed to hold the entire apparatus together.

His mouth went dry. Dear God. He could only imagine how they would look on Wendy.

She made a face. "Too much? You're probably right." She sighed and put the thong back. "Besides, I'm wearing one almost like it." She wagged her finger at Nate. "You have to keep reminding me that I'm looking for serious underwear." She picked up a black bra with no cups and a pair of pink ruffled panties. "I mean, I have all of this stuff at home." With impatient movements, she rehung the items, then walked toward a rack that held more substantial fare.

Nate shuffled after her, still trying to digest the fact that the only thing between the demure navy dress and Wendy's nakedness was a ribbon the size of a blade of grass. And that apparently her lingerie drawer was a treasure trove.

His cock began to swell.

"How about this?" she asked, holding up a utilitarian beige bra with wide straps. There were no concessions to femininity, no bows, no lace.

He opened his mouth to say that it looked like something his mother would wear, and then it hit him—her boyfriend would *hate* it. "I think it's great," Nate said, nodding. "Very…classy."

She brightened. "You think?"

"Absolutely."

From the rack she pulled a pair of bloomers that looked as if they would cover her from neck to knees. "I'll need a matching set."

"Right," he agreed.

"Would you like to try those on?" a saleswoman asked Wendy.

"Yes, I would," Wendy said.

"Right this way, sir," the woman said, gesturing for Nate to join them. "We have a private dressing room where you can view the clothes."

He felt himself blanch. "Uh…"

"Come on, Nate," Wendy said, rolling her hand. "You said you'd give me your opinion."

His feet were anvils. But one other part of his body was moving.

Nate was torn. He shouldn't join Wendy in the dressing room—it wasn't decent.

On the other hand, she wanted his opinion, and honestly, he'd seen her in bathing suits that were more revealing than the granny get-up she'd taken to try on.

Resolved to be a good friend, Nate strode after her.

The saleswoman let them into a private dressing room in which every surface was pink, then closed the door behind her when she left. Wendy winked at him, then disappeared behind a curtain. Nate swallowed hard and lowered himself gingerly to a pink bench, wondering how he was going to get out of this situation with his dignity intact. His erection already made it painful to sit.

Nate glanced up at the curtain and nearly fell off the bench. It was practically transparent. Behind the filmy barrier, Wendy was in silhouette, unzipping her dress.

He knew he should look away, but he couldn't. She stepped out of her high heels, then lifted the dress over her head. While he stared, transfixed, she unhooked her bra, allowing her breasts to fall forward. The hardened points of her nipples were clearly outlined.

He vividly remembered teasing her the day she'd gotten her training bra, saying that she was so flat it didn't matter. Then within a few weeks, she had blossomed right before his eyes, rounding out like ripe fruit. The experience had left him tongue-tied and a little nauseous.

Like now.

Nate exhaled forcefully and straightened one leg to get some relief.

But when Wendy bent over to step out of her red thong and it fell on the pink rug at her feet, he almost came on the spot.

Nate grunted and sprang up from the bench.

"Are you okay out there?" she called.

"Yeah," he said hoarsely. He looked away from the curtain, then dragged his hand down his face.

And looked back.

She was pulling the panties up her long legs and over the curve of her rear. The elastic snapped in place around her waist. Then she picked up the practical bra and harnessed her generous breasts. By the time she adjusted the straps, Nate was practically panting.

"Are you ready for me to come out?" she called.

Nate whirled to stare at the opposite wall, desperately trying to will away his hard-on. "Sure," he said in his best attempt at nonchalance.

The zip of the curtain being thrown aside made him

flinch. This wasn't right. Wendy had asked him to come because she assumed his interest in her was platonic. She had no idea how his mind and body had raged for her over the years. It wasn't fair of him to take advantage of the situation simply to ogle her.

"Nate?" she asked behind him.

"Yeah?" he said over his shoulder.

"Aren't you going to tell me what you think?"

He closed his eyes, wishing he had the strength to resist looking, but hadn't he dreamed of this moment countless times over the years while enduring the pain of seeing her leave her house with other guys?

"Nate?"

He took a deep breath and turned slowly…then his jaw went slack.

If he lived a hundred years, he would never forget the sight of Wendy standing in the threshold of the dressing room, with the light at her back, illuminating her figure to eye-watering perfection.

She held her arms over her head in a coquettish, pinup pose that highlighted her hourglass figure and long, long legs. Indeed, while the severe bra and full-coverage panties were demure in style, their flesh-tone color made it easy to imagine her completely nude.

As if his mind hadn't already been there a thousand times.

"What do you think?" she asked. "Does it give the right impression? That I'm a good girl?"

Realization slammed into him. She was doing this for another man. She didn't expect Nate to see her as a woman. Didn't expect him to even react like a man. Did she think he was a eunuch? Was he so pathetic to her?

"He'll love it," Nate heard himself say in a strangled voice.

She smiled. "You really think so?"

He managed to nod, then cleared his throat and averted his gaze. "I just got a call from the office—I have to go. Sorry about lunch."

Then Nate turned and walked out.

5

WENDY SAT STARING AT THE decimated white chocolate cheesecake. She'd started picking at it while waiting for Nate to get home and now all that was left to indicate what had once sat on the cardboard round were a few crumbs, and lines to show a server the size of an average portion.

As if.

Wendy tossed down her fork in surrender. She was officially depressed. So far, her plan to seduce Nate had failed miserably. She'd hoped the incident in the lingerie dressing room would end in them having "lunch" in a hotel room. Instead, Nate had walked out and had studiously ducked her and her phone calls since, responding to her questions about his coworker's party via clipped e-mails. Her behavior had obviously embarrassed Nate to death.

So much for convincing him she was ready to settle down.

She pulled out her BlackBerry and sent a text message to the other members of the Red Tote Book Club.

Operation Fanny Hill not going well. I just ate the
cheesecake I was going to bring to our next meeting. Help!

Within a few minutes, her handheld started to chime.
Don't quit now! Cassie Goodwin texted.
Raise the stakes, Page Sharpe sent.
What would Fanny do? Jacqueline Mays offered.

As Wendy expected, she didn't hear from Carol Snow.
But the other members had all made good points...

If she quit now, she wouldn't have Nate *or* the boyfriend she'd manufactured.

But things couldn't continue as-is—she had to raise
the stakes.

As far as what Fanny herself would do if she were
transplanted into contemporary times, she certainly
wouldn't shrink from her sexuality.

At the familiar sound of Nate's garage door going
up, Wendy's pulse spiked. She pushed to her feet and
walked out on the back porch to wait until he emerged
from the free-standing garage. She smoothed a hand
over the long sand-colored linen dress she wore.
Trading wardrobe items with Page Sharpe had served
them both well—Page needed to sex up her closet for
her seduction, and Wendy needed to downplay hers.

Nate was devastatingly handsome in his suit, carrying his black briefcase. He glanced up and, to her
dismay, his mouth tightened when he caught sight of her.

Wendy almost lost her nerve. She couldn't stand the
way Nate wouldn't look at her. "Hey," she said.

"Hey."

Wendy nodded to her house. "I have food samples

inside to choose the menu for your friend's party. It's enough for dinner."

His dark eyes narrowed at her drab dress. "You're not having dinner with Dalton?"

She shook her head. "He's…out of town. This would be a good time to cross a to-do item for the party off the list. We only have two weeks, you know."

He hesitated, then massaged the bridge of his nose. "Okay. Give me a few minutes to change."

Relieved, Wendy went back into her house. But her mind clicked away for what else she could be doing to prove to Nate she could change her ways, settle down to be a one-man woman.

Don't quit now… Raise the stakes… What would Fanny do?

She chewed on her thumbnail, mulling the possibilities until an idea slid into her head. A smile curled her mouth, then she sprinted upstairs to her bedroom.

NATE TOOK HIS CUSTOMARY seat at the Trainer dining room table where he'd been sitting for as long as he could remember. He and Wendy had traded off when they were kids, eating at his house one night, and at her house the next night. The shared dinners had dwindled when they'd entered their teens, though, because more often than not, Nate would come over to find Wendy's current boyfriend occupying his chair.

"You sure you don't need some help?" he called in the direction of the kitchen.

"I've got it all under control" came the muffled reply.

Nate leaned back in his chair to catch a glimpse of

her. The dress she wore revealed no leg, though…and she'd traded her platform high heels for flats.

He frowned. All for this Dalton character? To prove that she was no longer making herself available to other men?

Wendy walked in, balancing two plates of food on her arm. Nate reached to help, and studied the woman he'd known his entire life. Something was different, all right. The pinch between her eyes—a sign of stress, alien to the carefree Wendy. Was she so worried that this new man in her life wouldn't like her? She had certainly toned down her personality, and her appearance.

When she sat down across from him and smiled, Nate's heart did a flip-flop, like it first did back when her smile had revealed missing front teeth. It was her secret weapon, that smile.

Because of that sexy smile, clothes and lingerie that might look matronly on someone else wound up looking provocative on Wendy.

"You look hungry," she teased, laying her napkin across her lap.

He was…for her. But she was too consumed with another man to realize it.

"It smells great," he said, unfolding his own napkin. "What is all this stuff?"

"Barbecue pork tenderloin, Hawaiian chicken and sesame-encrusted tuna."

He cut a piece of the tenderloin, put it into his mouth, and groaned with pleasure. "Wow, did all of this come from the same place?"

She nodded. "My kitchen."

He laughed. "No, seriously."

"Seriously," she said with a pointed gaze. "I know how to cook—I just don't do it a lot. But that's about to change."

The fine piece of meat turned to sawdust in his mouth. "Let me guess—Dalton?"

She nodded dreamily. "I want to cook for him. Don't you think that will help him see me in a different light?"

"I…suppose so," he murmured, at a loss to explain this new side of her.

And the new side of him—he'd spent hours on the Internet looking for someone in the local landscaping scene whose name was Dalton, with no luck. He told himself all he had to do was ask Wendy for the guy's last name, but he hated for her to think that, frankly, he was doing exactly what he was doing.

Checking up on the guy.

"It's weird, but I think I'm going through a nesting phase," she said. "Today I actually got the urge to make curtains—can you believe it?"

Nate set down his utensils to concentrate on swallowing. Cooking. Nesting. It sounded as if she was trying to prove that she was *wife* material. His heart thudded in his chest. "Wendy, how did you meet this guy?"

She hesitated, then shrugged. "I don't remember. He's just always been around, a friend of a friend."

"So you've always known him, but you just now decide that you're in love with him?"

She nodded. "Crazy, isn't it?"

Instead of replying, Nate busied himself cutting another piece of meat while he nursed wounded pangs of jealousy. Why couldn't Wendy have fallen for *him*, the other guy who'd always been around?

He was quiet as she brought out more delicious courses of food for him to try. She had truly outdone herself—it was a shame that his appetite had vanished. Afterward he offered to help clean up, but she insisted she wanted to do it by herself and shooed him toward the back door. All he could think about was that she was willing to change her whole lifestyle for this new man in her life.

Nate looked at her shining face and agreed with something she said even as his heart squeezed with anguish.

He only hoped the guy was worth it.

When he stood at the back door saying goodbye, Wendy placed a box in his arms. He nearly buckled from the weight of it. "What's this?"

"Weren't you listening?" she admonished. "I asked you if you'd be willing to take these things off my hands."

"What things?"

She lifted the lid. "My sex toys. I don't want Dalton to find them and think…you know."

Nate looked down into the box of paraphernalia, seeing lubricants of every flavor, vibrators of all sizes, condoms in every color, plus feathers, handcuffs, a blindfold, a riding crop and numerous manuals on sex positions, sex games and tantric sex. His cock instantly hardened. "Uh, yeah…I know."

Wendy leaned forward and kissed him on the mouth, but by the time he registered her lips on his, it was over. "Thanks, Nate. You're the best." Then she closed the door in his face.

Nate limped home and by the time he'd climbed the steps to his bedroom, his cock was aching for release. He set down the box and unzipped his pants, freeing his erection with a groan of relief. Wendy had had him tied in knots all evening. And that goodnight kiss…who needed a box of sex toys to get off when he had the memory of her mouth on his?

Nate stroked his cock and, almost immediately, felt an orgasm building in his sack. He tried to prolong the release, but the barrage of images of Wendy was too powerful to ignore. His orgasm was loud and forceful, leaving him weakened and satisfied momentarily. But afterward, Nate conceded that he might never be truly satisfied unless he could experience an orgasm with Wendy, lying with her, looking into her eyes, belly to belly.

But Wendy had resisted his advances since he was old enough to make them. And hadn't she made it clear that she was in love this time, and not with him?

Nate opened a drawer and removed a cherished keepsake, a scrapbook that Wendy had given him when they graduated high school. Since that time he'd kept it updated, although there were fewer and fewer pictures of them as time went on. Still, photos told their story of growing up next to each other, playmates, best friends, confidants. But not lovers.

They would never be lovers.

Nate closed the book and paced the floor, wrestling with the hardest decision of his life. After an hour of wearing out the carpet, though, his mind was made up.

It was time for him to move on. Time to accept the firm's offer to relocate to the Boston office. Time to sell the house that he'd bought to remain close to Wendy. Time to begin the process of getting over her.

Wendy Trainer was the love of his life…and she would never know.

6

"GREAT PARTY."

Wendy jumped at the sound of Nate's voice in her ear, then she turned to drink him in. He'd been scarce for the past two weeks, traveling to Boston on business. She'd missed him desperately and feared he might have visited his old girlfriend to pick up where they'd left off.

God, she loved this man.

Wendy lifted the end of his tie. "I was wondering if you were going to make it."

Nate winked. "Wouldn't miss it." He glanced around. "Did you bring Dalton?"

"Um, no."

He looked disappointed. "I was hoping to get to meet him before—"

Wendy frowned. "Before what?"

"Before the party," he said easily. Then he swept his arm toward the crowd and the food tables. In the corner a slide slow of pictures of the senior partner's career played on continuous loop. "You did a great job. Harold and his wife are really pleased with the send-off."

"Are *you* pleased, Nate?"

He looked surprised. "Of course I am. I'm so proud of your success, Wendy."

At his warm words, her heart welled. She compared it to Fanny Hill's moment of achieving acceptance and silently thanked the late John Cleland for creating the spunky character of Fanny Hill to inspire her.

"So I look presentable?" Wendy teased, lifting her hands to do a little half-turn. She'd spent hours on her conservative suit, hair and makeup to achieve an understated look.

Appreciation lit his brown eyes as he skimmed her figure, then he leaned in. "You look great. But personally, I prefer Wendy the wild child, with the impossibly short skirts and the unruly hair."

Shock bolted through her. Nate preferred her the way she was before? She'd gone through this transformation for nothing? Then she stopped and reminded herself that "preferring" was a long way from being in love. Perhaps he simply meant that she was more fun before…or that he'd known what to expect from her.

Before she could respond, one of the senior partners stepped to the microphone and asked for quiet so he could say a few words about the guest of honor. Everyone listened, laughing and applauding in the right places, then raised their glasses to the retiring partner.

"And one more thing, if I may," the senior partner said, silencing the crowd again. "I'd like to announce that one of our favorite partners in the Atlanta firm, Nate Bertram, will be leaving to join our Boston group. A toast to Nate—he will be missed."

All around Wendy voices chorused, "Cheers," and glasses clinked. Several people close by shook Nate's hand or clapped his shoulder in congratulations, but she seemed to be rooted to the spot, her smile frozen.

Nate was leaving her? Her heart shuddered. How would she bear it?

When he was free, Nate turned to look at her, his dark eyes merry. "No congratulations?"

"Congratulations," she said woodenly. "How soon…" She had to stop to catch her breath. "How soon will you be moving?"

"I have to go back to Boston tomorrow. The movers will take care of everything."

Her lungs squeezed painfully. "That soon? What about the house?"

He lifted his hands. "I didn't even have to put a sign in the yard. When the real estate agent heard the address, she made a couple of phone calls and I got an offer."

Wendy groped behind her, grateful to find the wall close enough that she could lean into it versus falling down. "You're selling the house?"

He nodded. "I'm sorry I didn't get to tell you about everything before the announcement was made."

"I understand," she murmured. But she didn't. How could Nate make a decision like that without telling her? Easy—because she wasn't the woman in his life. "I guess you and Suzanne are getting back together?"

"It's Susan," he corrected.

Wendy nodded calmly, but inside she was dying. She'd missed her chance, waited too long to tell Nate how she felt about him. And she had no one to blame but herself. She felt as if the floor had fallen away, leaving her hanging, like she'd left Nate hanging when they were younger.

"Hey…are we good?" he asked, his face lined with concern.

Wendy realized it was up to her to make sure their relationship ended on an up note, so she manufactured a smile. "We're good. And the party is almost over. How about one last night on the town with an old friend?"

He grinned. "I think that sounds terrific."

"I want to change," Wendy said, her pulse clicking in anticipation. Tonight was her last chance to seduce Nate. "Pick me up at home in an hour?"

"I'll be there."

7

NATE BYPASSED THE BACK door of Wendy's house and knocked on the front door instead. Maybe it was silly, but he'd waited all these years to take Wendy out on a date, to be the guy who walked up to the front door. This night would be his last memory of Wendy, and he wanted everything to be perfect.

As perfect as things could be with her being in love with another man.

He nursed a few pangs about misleading her into thinking he and Susan were getting back together, but he did have his pride. She had Dalton, after all.

Nate had a moment of panic that Wendy might bring her boyfriend along since Nate had opened his big mouth and said he'd like to meet him. But when Wendy opened the door, to his relief, she was alone.

And she had on a red tube dress for which the manufacturer had apparently run out of fabric—on both ends. What she was *not* wearing under the dress was the matronly underwear…in fact, it looked as if she wasn't wearing underwear at all. Her white shoes had ridiculously high heels. And her blond hair was a luminous riot around her face and shoulders.

She looked spectacular.

"Hi, Nate," she said, beaming. "You look handsome. Ready?"

She didn't give him a chance to bask in her praise, just pulled the door closed behind her and walked to the car in those impossible heels.

Nate was so spellbound he almost didn't make it to the car in time to hold open her door. She chattered all the way to Buckhead, where all the trendiest clubs were located. Once they arrived at a destination spilling with people and throbbing with music, she knew the valet *and* the doorman.

She dragged Nate into the teeming place and stopped only to order a martini at one end of the bar and pick it up at the other end before progressing to the dance floor where she proceeded to move her amazing body with the enthusiasm of a teenager.

This was the Wendy he knew and loved, Nate acknowledged. Wild and uninhibited. Fearless. Happy. He hoped that Dalton would learn to appreciate her for who she was.

"Dance with me, Nate!" she shouted. Then she looped her arms around his neck and pulled his body close to hers.

He was already hard for her, but the close contact electrified him. Bodies crushed them on all sides. She slid her hips against his in a sensual tease that made him crazy for her. In the back of his mind, he knew she would rather be dancing with the guy she was so nuts over, but he decided to be selfish for one night. Pure happiness filled him and he fantasized that when Wendy looked at him, she saw a desirable man instead of just plain old unexciting Nate.

They danced the night away. Mindful of having to drive home, Nate had only a couple of beers, but Wendy kept knocking down the martinis. At one point she pulled his head down and locked his lips on hers for a long, sensual kiss. He realized she was probably too tipsy to know what she was doing, but Nate seized the moment to explore her mouth as thoroughly as he'd always wanted to after they'd both gone through the awkward stage of braces.

Kissing Wendy was heavenly, just as he'd known it would be. Her mouth was sweet and plump, her tongue warm and insistent. He wanted it never to end.

She pulled back and stared up at him. "Let's get out of here."

He swallowed hard. "Where do you want to go?"

"Take me home and make love to me in my bed."

At first Nate thought the loud music had distorted her words. "Say again?"

She leaned into him, crushing her full breasts against his chest. "Take me home, Nate, and make love to me in my bed." Her big blue eyes were hooded, her features soft with desire. Lust pumped through his body like a drug.

Not trusting himself to answer, he clasped her hand and led her off the dance floor and through the throng of people to wait for their car. Throughout she clung to his hand and rubbed his arm. When they were in the car, she let her fingers trail over his thigh. Neither of them spoke. The tension was palpable.

Nate kept telling himself that by the time they arrived home, she would change her mind. When he parked his car and walked her to her door, he was prepared for her to give him a requisite hug and friendly kiss on the cheek. She walked inside, then turned back. "Aren't you coming in?"

"Wendy," he murmured, then wiped his hand over his mouth. "Are you sure about this?"

She angled her head. "Why not, Nate? We're both curious about what it would be like to sleep together. And this will be our last chance to…experiment."

His hands were fairly shaking from wanting to touch her, but he had to ask. "What about Dalton?"

An unreadable expression came over her face. "This has nothing to do with Dalton. It's just sex. What about Susan?"

Nate bit down on the inside of his cheek. Even though he knew Wendy would never feel the way about him that he felt about her, her casual words cut him deep. Still, on the eve of leaving her, he would take what he could get. "Like you said, it's just sex."

Was it his imagination, or was that hesitation in her eyes?

A heartbeat later, though, any indecision was forgotten when she pulled him inside. She kissed him and walked him toward the stairs in the dark. It was a good thing, Nate acknowledged, that he knew the layout of her house as well as he knew his own.

His vital signs were going haywire. Aside from the exquisite feel of her body against his and her hands roaming over his back, this was Wendy, the woman who had fueled his wet dreams and teenage fantasies and manhood desires.

He kept telling himself that by the time they reached her bedroom, she would change her mind, but when they reached the stairs, she started to undress.

Good God.

Off came the high heels, thudding to the floor. Then the dress. He was right that she hadn't been wearing a bra. When her naked breasts spilled into his hands, Nate groaned, nearly overcome to be touching her like this. She pulled at his clothes, undoing, ripping and discarding. By the time they made it to the top of the stairs, he was wearing only his boxers, and she, a tiny triangle for panties. Light filtering through a window on the landing illuminated her body.

"You're beautiful," he murmured, then pulled her close for another searing kiss. He palmed her breasts and squeezed her nipples. She moaned and arched into him, then she slid her hands inside the waistband of his boxers and wrapped her fingers around the length of his erection. Nate gasped.

"I knew you would be big," she murmured against his neck. She kissed her way down his chest and stomach, but when Nate realized her destination, he stopped her.

"Not now," he said through gritted teeth. "Not yet. I'm barely hanging on here."

He picked her up and carried her to her bedroom, which, other than décor, had changed very little since they were kids. She could've used the master suite in her parents' absence, but he was glad she was still sleeping in the same room. How many times had he dreamed of joining her on this bed to do something more than watch TV or study?

Nate crossed the room in two strides, then lay Wendy's nearly naked form on top of the cover. She lifted her hips and shimmied the miniature panties down her legs. Then she smiled and tossed them to him.

He lifted the silky scrap of fabric to rub against his cheek, then inhaled the sultry scent of her into his lungs. He stood at the foot of the bed to soak in every detail, to brand the image of her into his brain so he could call up this memory in the years to come. She lay with her arms above her head, her golden hair fanned around her. Her full breasts were thrust in the air, the tips hard and distended. Her narrow waist flared to rounded hips. And at the intersection of her long, lean legs lay the exquisite nest that had pretty much dominated his thoughts since the age of thirteen.

Nate felt as if everything in his life had been building to this moment....

FROM THE BED, Wendy stared up at Nate, wondering if he had any idea how sexy he was, and how much she wanted him. As seconds ticked by on the clock on her nightstand, then a minute, she panicked that he was going to change his mind. Lifting herself on one elbow, she smiled. "After all this time, Nate, are you just going to stand there?"

His jaw hardened. "No."

She undulated on the bed, her knees parting involuntarily in invitation. He set aside her panties, then pushed down his boxers and crawled on top of her in practically one motion. He kissed her knees, then buried his face between her thighs and sank his tongue deep inside her.

Wendy gasped at the unexpected act of intimacy. The sensations that his mouth unleashed were further amplified by the fact that when she looked down, it was Nate pleasuring her. It was incredible, yet at the same time, it seemed so completely natural. Of course it was Nate doing amazing things to her—hadn't he looked out for her, taken care of her their entire lives?

An orgasm years in the making began to make its way to the surface. Even as she yielded to his tongue, she prepared herself, because she sensed a Nate-induced climax would surpass any sexual experience to-date.

Still…oh, God…she wasn't prepared for the groundswell of pure pleasure so intense that it claimed her body in a physical takeover. She drove her hands into his hair and dug her heels into the bed. A primal scream escaped her as the waves of bliss continued to break over her.

While her body still pulsed with the pleasure he'd given her, Nate lifted his head and inched up her body, stopping to sample her navel and the sensitive tips of her breasts. She wrapped her arms and legs around him, desperate to feel the weight of his body on hers.

"Nate…please," she whispered. "I need you inside me…now." She pointed to a nightstand. "There are condoms in the drawer." Thank goodness she hadn't given him all the condoms when she'd given him the box of sex toys.

He retrieved a condom and sheathed himself, then lowered himself to the cradle of her thighs. Nate cupped her face in his hands and locked her gaze with his. Then he shifted his body to position his rigid staff at the entrance of her slick channel and entered her in one long thrust.

Wendy inhaled sharply at the jarring fullness of Nate's body imbedded in hers. He groaned, stilling to give them both time to adjust to the comingling of their bodies. They were the perfect physical complement…it was as if she had been searching all her life for a puzzle piece that eluded her…and all along it had been next door. The sheer wonder of it left her speechless.

Nate continued to look into her eyes as he moved his hips to find a slow, deep rhythm. His jaw was hardened in restraint. She allowed him to set the pace, meeting him stroke for stroke, milking him with her inner walls. The torture was exquisite. Then, incredibly, she felt another orgasm building in her belly.

She clutched at his shoulders and hips as the climax caught fire and blazed a trail through her body. Her contractions seemed to escalate his own orgasm. His hips pumped furiously, and they came together, their bodies arched in supreme exertion. Nate's guttural cry echoed off her bedroom walls, testament to the force of his release.

Overwhelmed, Wendy could only relax into the mattress and steep in the magic they'd created. Nate eased forward on her chest, dropping kisses on her breasts and neck. His satisfied sigh resonated in her ear, but could not overshadow his agreement that this was only sex, a culmination of years of flirtation. She gathered him against her to ward off the sadness she felt infringing on this remarkable moment.

Making love with Nate was everything she thought it would be. Including the part where he didn't love her.

8

NATE STOOD AT THE WINDOW of his bedroom, looking across to Wendy's house in the pre-dawn light. Her bedroom window was open, a white sheer fluttering out on a summer breeze, beckoning him.

Leaving her bed in the wee hours of the morning was the hardest thing he'd ever had to do. Their night together was…staggering.

At least to him.

To Wendy, though, it had simply been sex, the fulfillment of a fantasy before he left town for good. A pang of remorse struck him for being weak. He'd promised to support her efforts to settle down in an effort to commit to Dalton, and instead, like every other man who'd ever crossed Wendy's path, he'd jumped at the opportunity to crawl into her bed.

He turned back to the room and checked his watch— fifteen minutes until he had to leave for the airport.

Nate glanced around the room that held so many good memories. In a few days, the movers would come and strip its contents to ship to him, and the new owners would come through to paint it some designer color for a guest bedroom or office.

His gaze landed on the scrapbook Wendy had made

for him. He walked over and thumbed through the pages, allowing the memories to wash over him. The two of them learning to rollerblade, the summer they'd both gotten poison ivy and the winter they'd both gotten chicken pox. Science fairs, new pets, scraped knees and homemade Halloween costumes—he and Wendy had been through it all together.

One of the last pages of the scrapbook held a photo of the two of them at their college graduation, in caps and gowns. They had their arms around each other, but only Wendy was looking at the camera.

He was looking at her.

From the raw adoration on his face, it must have been clear to anyone with eyes that he'd been head over heels in love with her. But in the photo, Wendy was oblivious. In fact, she was holding up two fingers behind his head—the universal sign for "jackass."

And nothing had changed, Nate realized miserably. He'd thought that sleeping with Wendy would help to exorcise her from his heart, but instead, it had only embedded her that much deeper. Meanwhile, she would go on with her life just as if the earth hadn't moved last night.

Nate unzipped his suitcase to place the scrapbook inside. When it wouldn't fit, he decided to carry it onto the plane. Rewinding through memories would help to pass the flight. And maybe by the time he landed in Boston, he would have regained his equilibrium.

He closed the curtains, picked up his suitcase, and walked through the house he loved for the last time. Finally, he exited through the back door and headed toward the garage. Then, on a whim, he detoured to the sprawling tree he and Wendy had loved to climb when they were kids. For some unknown reason, it suddenly felt very important to find the initials they'd carved into the tree. He needed to know that a permanent record of their friendship would always remain.

WENDY SAT WITH HER BACK against the trunk of the tree she and Nate used to climb, watching the sun rise, when she heard footsteps approach. She peeked around to see Nate walking up, wearing jeans and a dress shirt, his hair still damp from the shower. Her heart somersaulted at the sight of him. When she'd woken up in the middle of the night to find him gone from her bed, she'd been bereft. Her body still sang from his attentive lovemaking. And her heart was breaking with the knowledge that just as she'd realized how much Nate meant to her, he was being snatched away.

He ran his hand over the bark of the tree, so intent on finding something that he didn't notice her.

She smiled when she realized he was looking for the initials they'd carved into the tree when they were kids.

"Look up and to the right," she said.

Nate jerked his head around. "Hey. I didn't see you." Then he glanced back to the tree. "I can just make them out. NB & WT."

"The tree tried to repair itself," she said, pushing to her bare feet, wishing she'd taken the time to slide into sandals. As she knocked dew-laden grass from her jeans, her pulse jerked erratically. She'd desperately hoped that last night had changed things between them, but Nate's suitcase was a definitive sign it hadn't.

He ran his hand over the faint impression in the bark. "Lots of memories here."

She pointed to the scrapbook he held under his arm. "Can I see?"

He handed it to her. "Guess I was feeling sentimental this morning."

She flipped through the pictures, smiling every few pages. "I'm surprised you kept this. You even updated it, I see."

"Why are you surprised?"

She shrugged and handed it back. "I don't know. I guess I didn't think it would be that important to you."

"Wendy, your friendship has been the most important relationship in my life."

She bit into her lip. "My friendship?"

Nate nodded and reached forward to caress her jawbone with his thumb. It took great restraint for her not to turn her face into his hand and kiss his palm.

"Were you going to say goodbye?" she asked.

He dropped his hand. "I thought it might be awkward after…last night."

Meaning he had regrets. "I understand," she said, putting on a brave face. "But promise me you'll call me when you get settled in Boston and let me know how everything is going."

"I promise," he said. Sadness flitted across his face. He would miss his childhood home, no doubt.

"Good luck with Susan," she added.

"Good luck with Dalton," he returned. He glanced at his watch and made a rueful noise. "I guess I'd better get going if I'm going to catch my plane."

She nodded, pinching herself on the back of her hand to keep a flood of tears at bay.

He leaned forward and kissed her on the forehead. She closed her eyes and inhaled the clean scent of him. By the time he pulled back, she had schooled her face into a smile.

"Goodbye, Wendy."

"Goodbye, Nate."

He glanced down at the base of the tree. "Don't forget your book."

Wendy followed his gaze to her dog-eared copy of *Fanny Hill.* She'd been planning to read it today after Nate left, to pass the time. But when she looked at the book, she was reminded of the charge to seduce the man of her dreams.

She'd done that…but it wasn't enough.

She turned to see Nate walking toward the garage, his stride purposeful. He seemed eager to go, to get to his new life.

But she couldn't let him go without telling him how she felt. Fanny would never give up on her beloved Charles, the one man among her many lovers who'd captured her heart, and neither would she give up on Nate.

"Nate!"

He turned back, a little frown on his face.

She slowly walked up to him, her heart in her throat, then planted her feet. "Don't go."

He squinted. "What?"

"Don't go." Wendy took a deep breath for courage. "I love you, Nate."

His mouth opened, then closed, then opened again. "I…don't understand."

Her shoulders dropped and she gave a little laugh. "What don't you understand about 'I love you'? I want us to be together."

He seemed flustered, at a loss for words. "How... when...what about Dalton?"

"There is no Dalton. Dalton is you."

Nate put a hand to his forehead. "I'm totally confused."

Wendy winced. "I made him up. I was trying to convince you that I was ready to settle down, but..." She wet her lips. "It's you I want to settle down with, Nate. I love *you*."

Nate took a step back, as if he'd been hit. Raw emotions played over his face—shock, disbelief...bewilderment. He turned his back and seemed to be struggling with how to respond.

Wendy's heart shivered with disappointment. He didn't feel the same way about her. He loved her, but he wasn't "in" love with her. Last night had been great, but it wasn't enough to base a relationship on.

Wendy exhaled slowly. Loving him meant letting him off the hook.

"On second thought," she said in a breezy tone, "scratch that. Forget I said anything...I know you'll be happy in Boston with Susan. Have a good life, Nate."

She turned around and as much as she wanted to sprint back to the house, lock the door and pull the shades, she somehow managed to calmly walk with her head in the air. Mortification bled through her chest, but she was determined that only the members of her book club would know how crushed she truly was.

"Wendy!"

She didn't turn around. What must Nate think of her? Did he pity her?

He snagged her arm. "Wendy."

She looked up at him, fighting tears.

"You forgot your book," he said, holding up her copy of *Fanny Hill*.

She swallowed hard and took the book. "Thank you." Then she turned back toward the house.

"And speaking of books," he said.

Wendy hesitated, then looked back to see him holding up the scrapbook she'd made for him.

He walked closer. "I was thinking...maybe we could add a new chapter to our book."

She frowned in confusion.

A smile curved his mouth. "Of course, that means I'd have to stay."

Her lips parted and her heart buoyed. "You'd stay?"

Nate nodded, then pulled her into his arms. He studied her face for so long, she began to feel self-conscious.

"I can't remember not loving you," he murmured. "But I never thought...and after last night..." He stopped, then shook his head and squeezed her tighter. "I can't believe this. You've made me the happiest man alive."

Her heart and body opened for him. Uttering happy little sounds, she pulled his mouth down to hers and devoured him. His hips moved against hers, his need for her blatant. When her body became feverish, she broke the kiss and pulled him toward her house. "Let's go to my bedroom."

But he pulled her toward his house. "No, let's go to mine."

"No, mine."

He grinned. "I have the box of sex toys."

"Okay, yours." Wendy laughed and followed Nate, eager to embark on the new chapter of their life story.

SURPRISE ENDING

1

JACQUELINE MAYS SAT IN A ROOM in the Atlanta Public Library for the monthly meeting of the Red Tote Book Club. And her mind was a million miles away.

Or at least ten miles away, up the road to the tony area of Buckhead.

How dare Elliot Nicholson stand her up! Didn't the smug restaurateur realize that as a tax inspector for the state of Georgia, she had the power to shut him down if he chose not to comply with the terms of the on-site audit?

Nicholson was a local celebrity chef. She'd seen him a few times on television—he had leading-man good looks, but a brooding personality. She'd been warned by her manager that Nicholson would be difficult—two other auditors had tried to work with him and had given up. The only reason the state auditor's office was bending over backward to accommodate Nicholson was because the head of the tourism board had asked Jacqueline's boss to be patient, that the man generated a hundred times more revenue for the state through his restaurant and cooking show than he could possibly have dodged in taxes.

But nothing rankled Jacqueline's sense of order and justice like someone who tried to evade the tax code simply because of their fame or notoriety. Jacqueline thrived on difficult cases—her record for closing audits quickly and efficiently was legendary. Around the office, she was known as Last Chance Mays. If she gave up on an account, the taxpayer was sunk.

She'd been looking forward to meeting the man at his fancy restaurant Bing and letting him know that she would not be tolerating the lax attitude that he'd shown to her predecessors.

Except he hadn't bothered to show up.

And no one on the staff seemed to know where he was. Jacqueline had left him numerous messages, all of which had gone unanswered. Finally, she'd given up and left a stern message that unless he returned her call, she would report him for non-compliance and he could deal with the state court system versus the state auditor's office.

Infuriating man.

"Jacqueline?"

She blinked and focused on the leader of the book club, Gabrielle Pope, who seemed to be waiting for some kind of response. "I'm sorry—what was that?"

Gabrielle's smile encompassed Jacqueline and the other four members of the Red Tote Book Club who sat around a table. Normally they would be discussing the merits of a classic erotic novel, but for the past three months, the members had been conducting their own seduction by the book experiment by attempting to seduce the man of their dreams by drawing upon the inspiration of a favorite book club pick.

"I asked if you'd decided whether to take part in the seduction assignment," Gabrielle said.

Her moment of truth, Jacqueline acknowledged. She toyed with the stem of the wine glass which she'd nearly emptied.

"You know, of course, that the exercise is optional," Gabrielle murmured.

"Right," Jacqueline said. She pressed her lips together and glanced around the table at the faces of the women she'd gotten to know well over the past few months—Cassie Goodwin, Page Sharpe, Wendy Trainer and Carol Snow. The conversations in this room about sex were straightforward and uninhibited. No one ever passed judgment or criticized.

Of course, no one had admitted to the fantasy that she'd kept tucked away. Would everyone laugh? Think she was being archaic?

"I'd like to participate," Jacqueline said carefully, "but I don't have a target." She lifted her hands in a helpless gesture. "The story of my life—there's no man around when I need him."

The other members laughed and nodded in wry agreement. On the other hand, three of them had already reported success in their seductions.

"It's all about timing," Cassie offered.

"Do you at least have a book in mind?" Page asked.

A flush began to burn its way up her neck. Her mouth suddenly felt chalky. "I…rather liked… I mean… I felt a connection to the woman in…um…"

They were all looking at her expectantly.

"Go on," Gabrielle urged.

Jacqueline swallowed hard. "*The Slave* by Laura Antoniou."

There was a shocked pause during which no one

spoke. Eyes widened and gazes darted. Everything and everyone in the room seemed to be suspended.

"Outstanding," came Gabrielle's warm voice. "Would you like to share why?"

Jacqueline glanced at their leader, grateful for the opening and the encouragement. "I realize it's one of the most controversial books we read. I mean, the idea of a woman submitting to a man, wanting to feel pleasure-pain at his hands, flies in the face of being liberated and on equal footing with men."

Wendy cleared her throat. "I don't want you to take this the wrong way, but…you're such an accomplished, assertive woman, I admit I'm a little surprised."

Cassie leaned in, nodding. "If anything, it crossed my mind you might be a dominatrix." Then she looked stricken, as if she'd offended. "Not that there would be anything wrong with that…either."

Jacqueline looked at the expressions on the faces of the women around her. Instead of judgment, she found curiosity and eagerness to understand. Shot through with relief, she smiled and gestured to her severe suit. "You're right—I'm an aggressive woman, more assertive than many men I know. But when it comes to sex, I want to know there's a man out there who will take charge of my pleasure."

"I understand what you're saying," Page Sharpe offered. "My boss—my lover—says after making decisions all day at work, it's such a relief for someone else to take over."

Jacqueline nodded. "Except…it's more than just submitting to someone else's wishes." She wet her lips. "I want…that is, I crave…"

"You're free to speak your mind here," Gabrielle offered gently.

Jacqueline took a deep breath and blurted, "I've always wondered what it would be like to be restrained in some way...for a lover to lay his hands on me."

Cassie nodded. "My boyfriend and I have experimented with some light bondage. It's exciting."

Jacqueline relaxed a little. There was something about voicing a fantasy that was empowering. She gave a little laugh. "Okay, so I have the inspiration, and the fantasy...now if I could only find the man."

"Someone you used to date?" asked Cassie, who had successfully seduced a former boyfriend.

Jacqueline shook her head. "All married or otherwise unavailable."

"Coworker?" suggested Page, who was enjoying a love affair with her boss.

That made Jacqueline laugh. "I work with a bunch of out-of-shape accountants. Nice guys, but no potential there."

"How about a neighbor?" Wendy asked. Her seduction target had been the boy next door.

Jacqueline shook her head. "I live in midtown. All the single men in my building are gay." She sighed. "I guess I'll just have to wait until I cross paths with someone suitable—"

The vibration of her phone interrupted her. She glanced down to see the name and number of Elliot Nicholson flashing on the screen. Irritation flamed through her. "Pardon me—I need to take this call," she murmured, then excused herself to the hallway and stabbed the connection button.

"This is Jacqueline Mays," she said coolly.

"Elliot Nicholson here" came a smooth, smoky voice she recognized from television. "I'm supposed to call you?"

She frowned. "We had an appointment today."

A rueful noise came over the line. "Yeah—sorry about that. Something came up. But I'm at the restaurant now, so you're welcome to come by."

Jacqueline scoffed. "It's late."

A short laugh sounded. "My day's just getting started, lady. If you want to see me, you know where I am."

She opened her mouth to retort that she was no lady, then realized he'd hung up. "Ooh!" she muttered, putting away her phone. In normal circumstances, it was the responsibility of the person being audited to make himself or herself available. But Elliot Nicholson was obviously aware that he was getting special treatment and planned to milk it.

Jacqueline pursed her mouth. She wanted to see Mr. Nicholson in person, if only to let him know who he was dealing with now.

She returned to the meeting room and gave everyone an apologetic look. "I'm so sorry, but I have to leave. Duty calls."

They chorused regretful goodbyes. Jacqueline lifted her hand in a wave, then retraced her steps to exit the library and walk back to her car. With every step, her ire at Elliot Nicholson ratcheted higher. The arrogant ass, imposing on her free time when it was his business on the line.

Traffic was, of course, horrible. Summertime in Atlanta brought out tourists, suburbanites and cruisers.

It took her nearly an hour to traverse the short distance. Sitting in traffic at least gave her time to make sure every hair of her tight, dark chignon was in place, and the chance to freshen her deep red lipstick. While she blotted the color, she noticed her cheeks were pink and her eyes were bright—anger became her.

By the time she handed her keys to the valet at Bing, she had worked herself into a frustrated lather. The restaurant was crowded and noisy, adding to her discomfort. Lugging her bulky briefcase, she informed the hostess that Elliot Nicholson was expecting her.

"Mr. Nicholson is very busy," the young woman said, hedging.

"Where is he?" Jacqueline demanded. "In the kitchen?"

The hostess blanched and moved in front of Jacqueline, her hands lifted. "Yes, but no one is allowed to bother him while he's cooking."

Jacqueline glared at the woman. "Step. Aside."

The woman swallowed hard, then did as she was told. Jacqueline marched across the restaurant and through the swinging doors of the kitchen.

Chaos reigned. Bodies jockeyed for position. Plates of food were being prepared amidst shouting and juggling. The heat was oppressive. Sweet and savory aromas assailed her and her stomach growled, reminding her she hadn't eaten in hours. She moved through the crush, craning her neck to look for the man in charge.

She heard Elliot Nicholson before she saw him, recognized the voice, even though at the moment, it was at high decibels. "How many times do I have to tell you to always undercook the beef a little—it will be more tender. If it's too rare for the customer, we can always put it back on the fire. Once you've incinerated it, it's hard to go back, isn't it?"

Jacqueline turned the corner to find the man himself lecturing a younger chef on the art of preparing steak. Elliot Nicholson was a large man, tall and athletic, someone who would look more at home on a football field than in the kitchen of a 4-star restaurant. His hair was dark blond, his face tanned and strong, with a strong nose and square jaw.

Awareness niggled in Jacqueline's stomach. He was, in a word, gorgeous. On the heels of her observation, though, came the resentment that his good looks were one of the reasons the man was accustomed to getting his way.

The younger man holding the plate with the blackened beef nodded, cowering.

"Start all over," Elliot ordered. "And this time, do it right."

The man scurried away and suddenly Elliot noticed her standing there. He turned the full force of his gaze on her and scowled. "Who are you and what are you doing in my kitchen?"

But under the impact of his deep brown eyes appraising her, Jacqueline forgot her own name. Intensity and masculinity rolled off the man. But curiously, it was the large wooden spoon he held in one big hand that had her mesmerized. Long and hard and shiny, with a surface that looked as if it could deliver a stinging blow. Desire stirred in her midsection, but she finally found her tongue.

"I'm Jacqueline Mays." Her voice sounded amazingly strong and normal above the ruckus. "I'm auditing your restaurant financials."

His amazing mouth quirked into a frown. "I can't talk now."

"Mr. Nicholson," she said, adopting her most authoritative tone, "we have to talk sometime." When he didn't respond, she shrugged. "It's your restaurant. I don't mind if it's closed down for non-compliance of tax payments."

His scowl deepened. "I've paid every tax dollar I owe."

"You have to prove it to me," she reminded him. "That's why it's called an audit." She tried to focus, but her gaze kept straying to the wooden spoon and his white-knuckled grip on it.

His mouth tightened. "Come back tomorrow morning, nine o'clock."

"Okay," she said, then gave him her most stern look. "But this is your last chance, Mr. Nicholson." She turned around and walked out, feeling his dark-eyed gaze scanning her body like a hot beam.

When she exited the kitchen, she headed toward the ladies' room for a reprieve from the noise and to regroup. She sank into a chair in the lounge, and put a hand over her racing heart. Her cheeks burned and her breasts felt heavy with awareness. Elliot Nicholson was the most masculine male she'd encountered in a long time. His bigness, his maleness spoke to her. And the long, flat wooden spoon he'd wielded…

The thought of it making contact with her bare bottom made her sex tingle.

Jacqueline fumbled with her phone until she found the entry for text addresses for the book club group.

With shaking hands, Jacqueline punched in Target located. Seduction to commence.

Then, before she could change her mind, she hit the "send" button.

2

ELLIOT NICHOLSON METHODICALLY chopped vegetables for the day's meals. Cutting things into small pieces was satisfying and therapeutic, especially on days when he had to deal with extraneous, stupid details that fell outside of running the restaurant.

Like being audited, dammit.

The image of one Jacqueline Mays popped into his mind, her sharp hazel eyes boring into him, indicting him. He brought the knife down and actually saw the blood on the cutting board before he felt the sting of pain. He cursed and carried his finger to the sink to hold it under cool water. Thank goodness it was only a scrape.

"I thought you were supposed to wear gloves when preparing food."

He jerked around to see the woman he'd been thinking about standing there like a statue that had been set in place. Everything about her was precise, from her fine-boned features to her tightly bound dark hair to her little wire-rimmed glasses to the tailored skirt suit. Damn, but the woman had legs.

And his balls in her hand, if he believed her threat to close down his restaurant unless he cooperated.

"Good morning to you, too," he said dryly.

"I hope you aren't as lax about keeping financial records as you are about adhering to health codes."

He frowned, turned off the water, and reached for a towel. Then he took the cutting board of vegetables he'd been chopping and raked it all in the trash. "Happy? Believe it or not, I'm a stickler about food preparation." He leveled a glare in her direction. "And about my financial records."

"We'll see," she said, then made a clucking noise. She set her briefcase on a stool and glanced around the spotless kitchen.

Having worked in too many dirty food preparation areas, Elliot had vowed his would always be beyond reproach. The stainless steel countertops and the tile floor gleamed. He was sure she would find no fault there.

Not that her opinion of his restaurant or of him mattered, he reminded himself.

She wandered over to a container of utensils, pulled out a big flat wooden spoon, and caressed it with long, shapely fingers. Her casual familiarity with his favorite utensil irked him.

"Please don't touch my things," he said.

She arched an eyebrow in his direction and was it his imagination, or did her gaze jump down to his cock? When he realized how prudish he sounded, a flush singed his neck. The woman was about as repressed and cold as anyone he'd ever met, so why did she have him thinking in innuendo? And why suddenly did the idea of having his balls in her hand seem like not such a bad thing?

She returned the spoon to the container, then walked back to where he stood. "What time does the restaurant open?"

"Eleven," he said.

"And what time does it close?"

"We try to close the doors to customers around midnight. It takes a couple more hours to clean up."

"That makes for a long day."

"It doesn't leave much room for a social life," he agreed. A downside that he'd become more acutely aware of lately. He hadn't had a date in…well, if he couldn't remember, it must be a long damn time.

The woman was a beauty, he realized suddenly. Crystal clear features, and a tight bod. He wondered how long her hair would be if he released it from its bun…and if her ass was as shapely as it looked in that skirt. The pantyhose were a nice touch…so few women in Atlanta wore them because of the heat, but he loved the silky feel of them. He'd love to hold her slippery ass cheeks in his hands—

Elliot stopped and gave himself a mental shake. Where had that line of thought come from? The sooner this woman was out of his life, the better.

"So what am I supposed to do here?" he asked abruptly. "I've never been audited before."

"Simple," she replied. "You need to give me access to your financial records and either you or your Chief Financial Officer must be available to answer questions and provide documentation."

He closed his eyes briefly. That would be Lisa, the woman who had played with his heart and, he now suspected, with his company records. "My CFO left the company about six months ago, and I haven't found a replacement yet."

"Oh, well, your accountant will do. Or your book-keeper."

He straightened. "All inquiries will go through me." Now he insisted on knowing exactly how the restaurant's money was spent.

The Mays woman opened her briefcase and withdrew a piece of paper. "Very well. Here are the main concerns from the returns filed for the last three years. I need to see receipts and deposits and whatever other source documents you have to back up your forms."

"So I just have to answer these questions?" he asked.

"To start with," she said. "There might be more."

He scrubbed his hand over the back of his neck. "How long will this take?"

"That's up to you," she chirped.

As he took the papers, an alien feeling of helplessness came over Elliot. He'd built his restaurant from the ground up. He prided himself on maintaining control of every aspect of the business. He knew how many restaurants went belly-up due to poor management—he was determined it wouldn't happen to Bing. He only hoped it wasn't too late.

He glanced up at the cool, collected woman standing in front of him and fiercely wished he had some power over her, just to level the playing field. And then he remembered every woman's hot button.

"You're too skinny," he announced matter-of-factly.

Her brows furrowed in confusion. "I beg your pardon?"

"You could use a few curves," he said, walking around her to appraise her figure from all angles. He stared at her ass and made a mournful noise. "Yeah, you definitely need to be fattened up."

She gasped. "Confine your comments to the context of this audit, Mr. Nicholson."

But from the spots of color on her cheeks, he knew he'd gotten the upper hand. "This pertains to the audit," he said smoothly, then tapped the piece of paper she'd given him. "It's going to take me a couple of days to get my hands on all this stuff, so why don't I make you breakfast the day after tomorrow? We can go over the paperwork and you can enjoy some real food for a change."

"I'm not sure that would be appropriate," she murmured.

"Even better," he said, flashing a devilish smile that normally reduced women to a giggling mess.

But his smugness was short-circuited by the sudden glow of... Elliot's throat convulsed. Christ, was that *lust* in her hazel-colored eyes at the mention of inappropriate behavior?

Elliot's senses went on alert. He took in the slight parting of her lips, the dilated irises, the sudden increase in the rise and fall of her chest. He'd stumbled onto some kind of sensual trigger...

Unexpected desire bolted through him, rocking him back on his heels. Maybe there was more to the sterile auditor than he'd first realized....

3

JACQUELINE LOOKED OVER her shoulder and stared at her backside in the mirror. She flexed her glutes and frowned. Her ass wasn't that bad…was it? Medium-sized, she estimated, and moderately high, thanks to pilates. In fact, she'd always thought her butt was one of her best features.

The kind of ass a man wouldn't mind touching…grabbing…pinching…spanking.

Then she sighed.

Obviously it didn't impress Elliot Nicholson. Which did not bode well for her planned seduction, she admitted. Because while the man was as alpha-male as they came, and seemed to enjoy dominating just about every conversation and situation, if he didn't find her physically attractive, there was nothing she could do to convince him to take her in hand and bend her to his will.

She needed to regroup, figure out how to draw Elliot into her game.

Picking up a copy of *The Slave*, the book that had so inspired her, she reread one of the spanking scenes that always left her sex tingling. The scenes in the book ventured more into hardcore bondage and masochism than she cared to experience, but there were certain aspects of every scene that appealed to her…light restraint, lying in a submissive position and receiving swats from her lover's hands for some infraction.

Elliot had nice, big hands. She'd noticed when he was holding his injured finger under the running water. Thick, blunt-tipped fingers and giant palms…a good indication of how well the man was hung, she knew. But for the moment, she fantasized about those hands, so capable of delivering the right amount of pleasure-pain. Squeezing her nipples, being jammed inside her slick channel or massaging her buttocks.

A flush covered her entire body. She set down the book and tweaked her nipples until they were rosy and pert. From a box on her dresser she removed two nipple clamps and gently attached them, murmuring in pleasure at the slight zing of pain before her sensitive skin acclimated. Then she sank her fingers into the moist delta of her sex and began to massage her clit, sending ripples of pleasure drilling down deep into her womb. And all the while, she imagined Elliot Nicholson doing things to her with his amazing hands, applying just the right amount of pressure to bring her senses alive, then increasing the pressure until she couldn't endure it any longer.

"Yes," she encouraged him in her fantasy. "Harder… harder…"

When her climax claimed her, she cried out, her knees buckling. She was overcome with a rush of endorphins triggered from the twinges of pain. The high was addictive, and after she had recovered, she was struck immediately with the urge to do it again.

But she also knew the ultimate payoff in pacing herself, as well as the dangers in leaving the nipple clamps in place for too long. So she refrained from pleasuring herself again and hurried to get ready to meet Elliot for breakfast.

He was already a player in her game, even if he didn't know it. From now on, she lived to disobey him, in the hopes that he would become frustrated enough to take matters in hand, so to speak.

Fatten her up? Fat chance.

ELLIOT FROWNED AT THE food on Jacqueline's plate. She'd so mangled it with her fork, it was a disgusting hash of unnatural color. He looked up at the woman across from him. "Didn't anyone ever tell you not to play with your food?"

"What?" She moved her gaze from the report she studied, to her plate. "Oh…sorry, I guess I'm just not that hungry. It was tasty, though."

Elliot set down his own fork. "Tasty? Well, now, that's a glowing review."

"I'm not much of a foodie." She angled her head at him. "Which might explain why I'm skinny."

He was typically dismissive of people who didn't care about food, who didn't appreciate how much it affected every aspect of their life, from wellness to mood to sex drive. But the thought of tutoring this woman in the joys of food—the textures and the nuances of taste— excited him in a way he couldn't explain.

"Maybe I can teach you," he offered.

"I would be a good student," she replied, enunciating every syllable.

Elliot's adrenaline spiked. Did he imagine it, or had her voice vibrated with the sexy timbre of a double entendre? He stared at her across the table, his antennae raised for…what? He couldn't put his finger on this… tension that hung between them, tension that had nothing to do with the stresses of an audit. But there was something about this woman that made him want to assert himself. He wasn't the kind of man who was threatened by a beautiful, smart woman…but damn if she didn't have him thrown off-balance.

He'd thought about her nonstop the past two days, but didn't know why. It was just this elusive sense that despite her cool exterior, the woman was a live wire.

Or maybe it was just him fantasizing that he saw something repressed in this beauty that no other man could recognize…that no other man could coax to the surface. It was a self-inflating thought, that he alone had insight into this woman he barely knew. For one gut-clutching moment, Elliot wondered if it meant he'd bought into all the marketing hype about himself.

She finally looked back to the report, and he tried to shake the feeling that something was happening here other than the fact that his business might be in jeopardy. Wasn't that enough?

"How do the reports look?" he asked irritably.

"It's hard to say," she said noncommittally.

"When will you know?"

"I'm not sure."

Elliot sighed and tossed down his napkin. "Do you ever give a straight answer?"

She glanced up. "Mr. Nicholson, I can understand your frustration, but I didn't create this situation. I think you need an outlet for your anger."

Elliot stopped—there it was again…that timbre in

her voice…that flicker of sin in those amazing eyes of hers. Was she suggesting…? He swallowed hard and decided to hedge. "Any ideas, Ms. Mays?"

She pursed her mouth. "Actually, I've always heard that cooking is therapeutic. The stirring, the pounding… the whipping."

Under the napkin on his lap, his cock surged. "It… can be."

"Is there a particular station you like to work at?" she asked, gesturing to the whole of the kitchen.

At the innocuous question, he thought that, again, perhaps he'd misread her. "That one," he said, pointing.

She stood up from her chair and walked over to the work station he'd indicated. "The stainless steel is nice," she said, nodding, caressing the seamless surface. "Smooth….sleek…cool to the touch."

As he watched, she turned her back to him and leaned forward into the station slightly. With her high heels, the counter hit her perfectly to allow her to bend over the station. She reached for the container of utensils sitting in the center. In the process, her skirt rode up on the back of toned thighs.

And the pantyhose…

His cock swelled. Unable to stop himself, he stood and walked over to plant his hands on the counter on either side of her, pinning her in and enjoying the view of her ass mere inches away from his burgeoning erection. When she turned in the confines of his arms and angled body, she didn't react—didn't pull away, didn't melt into his arms. She held the same flat wooden spoon that she had fondled previously and gave him a cool smile.

"Does me being here make you angry, Mr. Nicholson?" She held the spoon in one hand and lightly swatted her other palm.

And suddenly it hit him…she was into some form of BDSM…it all fit—her severe look, her unnatural reserve…the fire he detected banked just below the surface. All that remained was figuring out which side of the equation she worked.

"Yes," he said honestly. "I don't want you here…I have other things I need to be doing."

"What else makes you angry?" she asked lightly, still swatting her hand.

"When customers send back perfectly good food," he murmured, playing along with her little game of Q&A.

"And what else?"

He noticed her eyes were growing slightly hooded, and that the intensity of the swats she gave her hand had increased. "What makes me angry," he said carefully, "is when people play with my food instead of eating it."

A little smile curved her mouth. "That was wrong of me, wasn't it?"

She was a submissive, he realized. And she wanted him to punish her for her bad behavior. As his body hardened, his mind raced, ticking through the logistics—they were alone and the entrances were locked. The manager had a key, but she wouldn't be in for at least an hour.

"Yes, it was wrong of you, Ms. Mays." He leaned in for a kiss, but she turned her head away. Instead, she handed him the spoon, her eyes glowing with anticipation. Then she turned and planted her hands on the table.

Elliot's cock was so rigid it was painful. He had no

idea what was expected of him, but he'd never been so turned on in his life. Moving on instinct, he pulled up her skirt to discover she wasn't wearing underwear with the sheer nude-colored pantyhose. Her ass was beautiful and shapely. The dark lips of her sex were visible through the hosiery. He almost came on the spot.

He took a deep breath for restraint, then he placed one hand on her left cheek and stroked the silky soft globe through the sheen of the hosiery. Heavenly. He hesitated, then brought the wooden spoon down on her right cheek. She squirmed a little, then murmured, "Harder."

He exhaled, then lifted the spoon and brought it down for a resounding smack. She recoiled, then groaned.

Encouraged, he did it again…and again…and again…

With each stroke, she flinched, then relaxed with a moan. Soon her buttocks glowed a bright pink, and the skin felt warm under his hand. Unaware how this was supposed to end, he took his cues from her.

"Faster," she murmured over her shoulder.

He obliged. And within a few strikes, she began to make the telltale noises of a woman on the verge of climax. He wanted to free his erection, yank down her pantyhose, and ram himself inside her, but he was out of his element here. So he kept spanking her with the spoon until she tensed and cried out, bucking toward the table. Watching her body convulse with an orgasm was a powerful thing, something he knew he'd never forget.

As her spasms slowed, so did his pace. When she stilled, he stopped altogether. His balls were full, and he was practically light-headed from wanting her. Struggling to think clearly, he waited for her to make the next move.

She took a few deep breaths, then straightened and, in slow, controlled movements, pushed down her skirt and smoothed a hand over the dark fabric. A strand of dark hair had escaped her tight little bun, but she tucked it back with an unhurried hand. Her face was schooled into a placid expression. "Thank you...for breakfast. Once I finish going over the reports, I'll let you know where we go from here."

Elliot stood flat-footed and open-mouthed as she picked up her briefcase and walked out, as if nothing out of the ordinary had transpired. Then he dropped into a chair, feeling as if he'd been hit by a truck. Reeling, he jammed his hand into his hair.

What had just happened?

And more importantly, how could he make sure it happened again?

4

JACQUELINE STUDIED THE new reports laid out before her, but she was aware of Elliot's gaze on her, as it had been since they'd met an hour ago. He'd made breakfast again, and she'd been careful not to play with her food. She'd avoided direct eye contact, except when absolutely necessary, and had kept the conversation on the business at hand. At this point, the audit could go either way. And while she was acutely aware that what she'd done could get her fired, she was also aware that Elliot Nicholson was intrigued. She could practically feel him straining toward her. Finally, he heaved a frustrated sigh.

"Don't you think we should talk about what happened the other day?" he blurted.

Jacqueline lifted her head. "The other day?"

He pursed his mouth. "The...incident. In here." He gestured to the table where she'd been bent over. "The...you know."

"The spanking?" she asked.

She enjoyed seeing the color bleed into his cheeks. "Yes," he said, finally.

"I made a mistake, you corrected me, that's all." She pointed to her plate where she had carefully left the portion of uneaten omelet intact. "See? I didn't play with my food."

He squinted. "And you do this often?"

"No. That was the first time."

His eyes widened. "First time? May I ask why you picked me?"

She shrugged. "I can't explain it. It had nothing to do with your celebrity, or this audit. I just looked at you and knew it had to happen. Haven't you ever felt that way about something? Compelled?"

He pressed his lips together, then nodded. "So…will it happen again?"

She gave another shrug. "I don't know. The audit is almost finished. Chances are, we'll never cross paths again." She was saying the words as much for herself as for him. Because even as she sat there pretending to be nonchalant, her bottom tingled to be lashed again. She glanced at his big hands and the urge increased tenfold.

Elliot pulled his hand over his mouth and stared at her, as if he were trying to figure out what made her tick. A beep from one of the stoves sounded. He pushed to his feet and walked over to stir something in a pot, then adjusted the gas flame lower.

"I need to make a quick phone call," he said, then gestured toward the pot. "Do you mind keeping an eye on this for me?"

"Not at all," she said.

He studied her, and looked as if he were going to say something else, but then turned and left.

Jacqueline expelled a long breath. Since the spanking session, she'd been plagued with indecision, much like Robin had had second thoughts in *The Slave* about throwing herself completely into a submissive life-style. She could still call it off—no body fluids had been exchanged.

Jacqueline pulled out her phone and frantically texted the members of the Red Tote Book Club. Afraid now that I've started, I can't stop. Am aborting the attempted seduction before I get in too deep.

She stared at her phone, hoping for feedback. A full six minutes later, her phone chimed to indicate a text message had arrived. Jacqueline was surprised to see it had come from Carol Snow, the loner in the group, the one person she'd least expected to hear from. She tabbed through and pulled up the message.

Glad to hear that you've come to your senses.

Jacqueline frowned, then became aware of a piercing noise.

She looked up just as Elliot ran back into the room. "The stove!"

The pot was on fire, and the piercing noise was the smoke alarm. She gasped and sprang into motion.

But Elliot was ahead of her, grabbed a fire extinguisher and used the stream of foamy powder to put out the flames. Then he used a broom to dislodge the smoke alarm that was still going off, and raised a window to allow the smoke to escape. He turned back to her, his eyebrows knit. "I asked you to watch the pot."

"I'm sorry," she stammered. "I was distracted."

"You could've been hurt. You could've destroyed the entire restaurant."

"I know," she said, her heart thudding in her chest at the close call.

He stalked toward her, his expression dark. Jacqueline's instinct was to back up, but he wouldn't let her get away. He pinned her against the same table as before and put his mouth next to her ear. "What should I do with you?"

Desire flooded her midsection, and a moan escaped her. "Punish me."

"How?"

She turned around and leaned over, offering her rear end.

"What am I supposed to use?" he asked. "I had to retire my favorite utensil." He reached for another tool. "Should I use a whisk? A rubber spatula?"

"Use your hand," she pleaded.

He yanked up her skirt and pushed it to her waist. The cool air on her bottom felt good because it was burning for his touch. She was wearing black pantyhose today, no underwear.

The swat of his hand took her by surprise, the vibration encompassing her sex. She moaned and undulated forward. But the second swat landed before she could recoil. After several solid strikes, she could feel her juices begin to flow. Suddenly, he yanked the pantyhose down, exposing her bare bottom.

"Is this what you want?" He leaned over to murmur in her ear.

"Yes," she moaned, lifting her ass higher in the air.

His hand landed against her bare skin in a solid smack that thrilled her to her toes. Again and again he paddled her, and occasionally his hand would brush the wet folds of her sex. It was ecstasy. She could feel a powerful orgasm building, faster and faster as the lashes continued in time with the excruciating pleasure coursing through her. When the climax hit her, she cried out and her knees buckled from the intensity. He had to support her to keep her from falling.

It was this last touch, this soft, protective touch that did her in. She would be bereft without him.

At the sight of her splayed before him, her beautiful ass cheeks, her glistening sex, Elliot was so wracked with lust, he could barely think. When she backed up into him and nudged his erection, he almost shouted in gratitude. He freed his aching cock and had the presence of mind to don a condom before grabbing her hips and thrusting into her with animalistic force. Her slippery walls tightened around him and their moans melded. With regret, he knew this wouldn't last long, and sure enough, within a few long, aggressive strokes, he could feel his body taking its own course. He slowed, but realized it was too late, then pounded into her, reveling in the sounds of their flesh slapping together. His orgasm was so explosive, it took his breath. All his muscles contracted and converged to expel the life seed out of him. He shouted in sheer rapture.

When the spasms finally receded, he could barely stand. He gently disengaged their bodies and leaned into the table. After a few seconds of recovery, he leaned over and whispered, "That was incredible."

Her response, though, was to wriggle out from under him, then straighten her clothes. "I'll be back tomorrow with the final audit report, Mr. Nicholson," she announced.

When she walked over to pick up her briefcase, he

lifted his hands in incredulity. "That's all you have to say?"

She turned her cool eyes back to him. "What did you expect?"

He hardened his jaw. "Nothing."

"Good," she said, then turned and walked out.

5

"WHAT'S THE VERDICT?" Elliot asked.

Jacqueline dropped her gaze to stare at two versions of the final audit report, torn. There were definite improprieties in the finances of Elliot Nicholson's restaurant, no doubt. And though they were numerous, they were all fairly minor. She had drawn up a version of the final report that included penalties of oversight that would mean she would be forced to spend more time with Elliot.

A notion that thrilled her to the core.

But she'd also drawn up another version, with penalties that could be paid discreetly and would require no further interaction between the two of them.

A notion that saddened her so much, it scared her.

She picked up her pen and looked back and forth between the two documents, aware of the pull of him from a few feet away. His body, calling to hers, calling her to submit, to put herself in his hands.

In the end, it was the fear, the realization that the first time she'd allowed herself to fulfill her lifelong fantasy, she'd put her ethics and job on the line, that made her reach for the alternate version, the one that guaranteed she'd probably never see Elliot again.

It was the right thing to do. Who knew what a hint of scandal might do to Elliot's commercial credit rating, or to employee morale, or even to his public persona? She couldn't risk it just to satisfy her subversive longings.

Jacqueline scanned the document, then signed and dated the bottom, and pushed it across the table to Elliot with a smile. "The state will be willing to settle for a small penalty that I think you'll find agreeable, Mr. Nicholson."

He held her gaze for a moment, then looked down at the document. But his shoulders didn't relax as much as she thought they might. "Okay," he said finally. "So that's it, then?"

She clasped her hands together and nodded. "That's it."

He set aside the paper and reached forward to cover one of her hands with his. "Look, Jacqueline, this is a little awkward, but I have to get this out." He moistened his lips. "I don't know exactly what happened between us or why…all I know is that I want it to continue…I can't get you out of my mind. I want to see you again."

She savored the way he'd said her name for the first time. She glanced at his hand covering hers and experienced a stab of desire just remembering that hand delivering erotic punishment to her body. If she saw him again, she'd have many chances to disobey…many chances to experience that ecstasy again.

Then she sighed in resignation. The seduction was over…and so was the game. Hadn't she proved to herself that she would risk everything for the thrill? She had to get out before anyone got hurt…before she did something irreparable to her reputation or to someone else.

"Elliot," she said carefully, "I don't think so. I'm sorry." She pushed to her feet and pulled her hand from beneath his. "Good luck with everything."

"Jacqueline, please reconsider. I want to explore this thing between us, see where it leads. Please."

She wavered, but it was the overwhelming desire to say yes that made her turn her back and walk away with a calm that belied her tripping heart.

In *The Slave*, Robin had been prepared to give up her life in order to indulge her fantasies of submitting to another. But Jacqueline wasn't that desperate...or that brave.

6

"VEAL CHOPS," Elliot yelled, sending a dressed plate down the sideboard to a waiting server. He pulled a bandanna from his pocket and mopped at his sweaty brow. Despite the air conditioning and several fans, the kitchen was hot as hell tonight.

"Boss, this is pork, not veal," the server said, extending the plate.

Elliot glanced at the meat on the plate, then winced. "My bad," he said. "Veal chops coming up."

He tried to blame the heat for his pervasive distraction, but in truth, it was Jacqueline Mays who had him so scattered that he could barely run his kitchen. His underchefs and servers covered for him, but he knew even they were tiring of his constant mistakes.

He threw himself into selecting the best veal chops he had on hand and preparing them to succulent perfection. Arranging them on a fresh plate with sweet potato fritters and arugula salad gave him a little stab of satisfaction. He sent the plate on its way, then wiped his brow again and exhaled noisily.

Eventually he'd forget her. Forget that she'd dive-bombed into his life, arriving long enough to set everything on end with erotic games that fueled his lust to unparalleled heights, then left just as unexpectedly as she'd arrived.

In the wee hours of the morning, he'd considered looking for her, but then doubts plagued him. What if his perceived connection with the woman wasn't real at all? What if this was her game, going from audit to audit, collecting erotic playmates, then moving on? He'd feel like a fool. And besides, hadn't she made it very clear that she didn't want to continue their relationship?

He could date plenty of other women, women who *wanted* to be with him.

So why was he fixated on this one woman with hazel eyes and dark hair and deep secrets?

"Boss," his server said with a sigh, holding up the plate of veal chops. "The customer at table eight sent back the veal. Said it's not prepared right."

Irritation barbed through him. "They're prepared perfectly," he barked.

The server raised a hand in apology. "I know. Sorry."

Something inside Elliot snapped. "I'll handle this." He took the plate and marched through the kitchen, out the swinging doors, and toward table eight. The customer wasn't *always* right…he would educate this ignorant patron how veal should be prepared and how it should taste. With every step, he seethed.

But when he got to the table, he came up short. And his heart buoyed.

Jacqueline Mays sat there, calmly sipping a martini. She raised her innocent gaze to his. "Hello, chef."

"Hello," he said, matching her casual tone. Then he held up the plate. "Did you order the veal?"

She nodded. "But I didn't like it."

"You know it makes me angry when customers return food."

"Yes, I'd heard that."

He leaned forward to whisper, "You're going to get it."

Her eyelids fluttered closed and her lips parted to release a little sigh. "Promise?" she murmured.

"I promise," he said against her mouth, then claimed a hard, hungry kiss. His hand swept lower to cup her behind. "Every night."

Jacqueline surged against his hand, her body ravaged with excitement. This was the way Robin must have felt when she decided to follow her fantasy, no matter where it led her.

It would be worth it.

Epilogue

GABRIELLE POPE GLANCED around the table at the five members of the Red Tote Book Club. Four of them—Cassie, Page, Wendy and Jacqueline—had drawn inspiration from the pages of the erotic novels they'd read as a group, and had succeeded beyond their wildest dreams in seducing the men of their choice. As a bonus, it seemed that in the process of pulling off a successful seduction, each of the four women had also found love.

The body language and expressions of the women were so different than only a few months ago when they'd first walked into the book club meeting, each hesitant and wary. Now they were laughing and relaxed, their conversations candid and supportive.

Cassie Goodwin glowed when she talked about how a sex chair had reignited the flame between her and an old boyfriend in ways they couldn't have imagined. The women had pored over pictures of the chair, discussing the practicality and beauty of a piece of furniture that was guaranteed to bring more to a relationship than a china cabinet.

Page Sharpe delighted in explaining that from nine

to five, she took direction from her boss, but after hours, she was definitely in charge. She had brought her exquisite faux fur coat to show the women and her new chic wardrobe reflected her new position at the firm and in her own psyche.

Wendy and her man were planning a wedding. The short courtship wasn't surprising considering the two of them had grown up next to each other, had known each other their entire lives. And since Wendy was a party planner, the event promised to be huge.

Jacqueline Mays wasn't the least bit shy to reveal the props she and her lover used when he dominated her in the bedroom. Elegant cuff bracelets became methods of restraint. And the women might never look at a wooden spoon in quite the same way again.

It was amazing what sexual confidence could do for a woman's soul, Gabrielle noted. The energy in the room was electric, the mood effervescent.

Gabrielle glanced to the end of the table.

With one exception.

Of the five members, only Carol Snow had refused to participate in their seduction by the book exercise. Yet Gabrielle sensed that the quiet, beautiful woman secretly yearned to connect with a lover. Maybe some past hurt was keeping her from seeking out companionship, or maybe she was simply too rigid to include someone in her life. Whatever the reason, Gabrielle hoped that Carol would someday recognize that life was better when shared with a loving partner, and that sex was a panacea for engaging the body, heart and mind.

Gabrielle touched a finger to her wrist to feel her own elevated pulse. She had high hopes for Carol because she herself had decided to take the plunge. From the beginning, she'd told herself that if some of the members could undertake a seduction and succeed based solely on chutzpah gained from reading a book, then she might try it herself.

Gabrielle was older than the other women by at least five years, and before the book club, had given up hope of ever finding a man patient enough to join her in pursuing a tantric lifestyle—intimacy of the highest level, an almost hypnotic state of bliss, if one were willing to surrender to the conscious art of loving.

But the fact that four out of the four women who had attempted a seduction had succeeded beyond their wildest imaginations, was encouraging, to say the least.

Maybe she still had a shot at her own happy ending after all...

"A toast," Wendy offered, lifting her wineglass, "to seduction by the book."

"Hear, hear," the other women chorused. Even Carol Snow joined in, which gave Gabrielle renewed hope.

"I think we should write our own erotic novel," Page suggested, and from the gasps of delight from the other women, Gabrielle realized the group had a new project.

Gabrielle had her own story to plan, and if she had her way, it would be way too hot to print.

But meanwhile, she could sit back and enjoy the camaraderie of the Red Tote Book Club and revel in the knowledge that she had brought these women together in the perfect intersection of sex, books and friendship.

Life was good…and would only get better.

* * * * *

Look for Gabrielle's story in
TOO HOT TO PRINT,
a special e-novella available in January 2010!
And don't worry about Carol—
she's going to get the sexily-ever-after
that's coming to her.
Don't miss Stephanie Bond's next Blaze book,
HER SEXY VALENTINE,
in February 2010.

*Celebrate 60 years of pure reading pleasure
with Harlequin®!*

To commemorate the event, Silhouette Special Edition invites you to Ashley O'Ballivan's bed-and-breakfast in the small town of Stone Creek. The beautiful innkeeper will have her hands full caring for her old flame Jack McCall. He's on the run and recovering from a mysterious illness, but that won't stop him from trying to win Ashley back.

*Enjoy an exclusive glimpse of Linda Lael Miller's
AT HOME IN STONE CREEK
Available in November 2009
from Silhouette Special Edition®*

The helicopter swung abruptly sideways in a dizzying arch, setting Jack McCall's fever-ravaged brain spinning.

His friend's voice sounded tinny, coming through the earphones. "You belong in a hospital," he said. "Not some backwater bed-and-breakfast."

All Jack really knew about the virus raging through his system was that it wasn't contagious, and there was no known treatment for it besides a lot of rest and quiet. "I don't like hospitals," he responded, hoping he sounded like his normal self. "They're full of sick people."

Vince Griffin chuckled but it was a dry sound, rough at the edges. "What's in Stone Creek, Arizona?" he asked. "Besides a whole lot of nothin'?"

Ashley O'Ballivan was in Stone Creek, and she was a whole lot of somethin', but Jack had neither the strength nor the inclination to explain. After the way he'd ducked out six months before, he didn't expect a welcome, knew he didn't deserve one. But Ashley, being Ashley, would take him in whatever her misgivings.

He had to get to Ashley; he'd be all right.

He closed his eyes, letting the fever swallow him.

There was no telling how much time had passed when he became aware of the chopper blades slowing overhead. Dimly, he saw the private ambulance waiting on the airfield outside of Stone Creek; it seemed that twilight had descended.

Jack sighed with relief. His clothes felt clammy against his flesh. His teeth began to chatter as two figures unloaded a gurney from the back of the ambulance and waited for the blades to stop.

"Great," Vince remarked, unsnapping his seat belt. "Those two look like volunteers, not real EMTs."

The chopper bounced sickeningly on its runners, and Vince, with a shake of his head, pushed open his door and jumped to the ground, head down.

Jack waited, wondering if he'd be able to stand on his own. After fumbling unsuccessfully with the buckle on his seat belt, he decided not.

When it was safe the EMTs approached, following Vince, who opened Jack's door.

His old friend Tanner Quinn stepped around Vince, his grin not quite reaching his eyes.

"You look like hell warmed over," he told Jack cheerfully.

"Since when are you an EMT?" Jack retorted.

Tanner reached in, wedged a shoulder under Jack's right arm and hauled him out of the chopper. His knees immediately buckled, and Vince stepped up, supporting him on the other side.

"In a place like Stone Creek," Tanner replied, "everybody helps out."

They reached the wheeled gurney, and Jack found himself on his back.

Tanner and the second man strapped him down, a process that brought back a few bad memories.

"Is there even a hospital in this place?" Vince asked irritably from somewhere in the night.

"There's a pretty good clinic over in Indian Rock," Tanner answered easily, "and it isn't far to Flagstaff." He paused to help his buddy hoist Jack and the gurney into the back of the ambulance. "You're in good hands, Jack. My wife is the best veterinarian in the state."

Jack laughed raggedly at that.

Vince muttered a curse.

Tanner climbed into the back beside him, perched on some kind of fold-down seat. The other man shut the doors.

"You in any pain?" Tanner said as his partner climbed into the driver's seat and started the engine.

"No." Jack looked up at his oldest and closest friend and wished he'd listened to Vince. Ever since he'd come down with the virus—a week after snatching a five-year-old girl back from her non-custodial parent, a small-time Colombian drug dealer—he hadn't been able to think about anyone or anything but Ashley. When he *could* think, anyway.

Now, in one of the first clearheaded moments he'd experienced since checking himself out of Bethesda the day before, he realized he might be making a major mistake. Not by facing Ashley—he owed her that much and a lot more. No, he could be putting her in danger, putting Tanner and his daughter and his pregnant wife in danger, too.

"I shouldn't have come here," he said, keeping his voice low.

Tanner shook his head, his jaw clamped down hard as though he was irritated by Jack's statement.

"This is where you belong," Tanner insisted. "If you'd had sense enough to know that six months ago, old buddy, when you bailed on Ashley without so much as a fare-thee-well, you wouldn't be in this mess."

Ashley. The name had run through his mind a million times in those six months, but hearing somebody say it out loud was like having a fist close around his insides and squeeze hard.

Jack couldn't speak.

Tanner didn't press for further conversation.

The ambulance bumped over country roads, finally hitting smooth blacktop.

"Here we are," Tanner said. "Ashley's place."

* * * * *

Will Jack be able to patch
things up with Ashley,
or will his past put the woman
he loves in harm's way?
Find out in
AT HOME IN STONE CREEK
by Linda Lael Miller
Available November 2009
from Silhouette Special Edition®

This November,
Silhouette Special Edition®
brings you

NEW YORK TIMES
BESTSELLING AUTHOR

LINDA LAEL
MILLER

Stone Creek

*Available in November
wherever books are sold.*

Silhouette
Desire

FROM *NEW YORK TIMES* BESTSELLING AUTHOR

DIANA PALMER

THE MAVERICK

A BRAND-NEW LONG, TALL TEXAN STORY

Silhouette

nocturne™

TIME RAIDERS
THE PROTECTOR

by *USA TODAY* bestselling author
MERLINE LOVELACE

Former USAF officer Cassandra Jones's unique psychic
skills come in handy, as she has been selected to join the
elite Time Raiders squad. Her first mission is to travel
back to seventh-century China to locate the final piece
of a missing bronze medallion. Major Max Brody is
assigned to accompany her, and soon Cassandra and
Max have to fight their growing attraction to each
other while the mission suddenly turns deadly....

*Available November
wherever books are sold.*

SN61822

SPECIAL EDITION

FROM *NEW YORK TIMES* BESTSELLING AUTHOR

Ashley O'Ballivan had her heart broken by a man years
ago—and now he's mysteriously back. Jack McCall *isn't*
the person she thinks he is. For her sake, he must keep
his distance, but his feelings for her are powerful.
To protect her—from his enemies and himself—he
has to leave...vowing to fight his way home to
her and Stone Creek forever.

Available in November wherever books are sold.

Visit Silhouette Books at www.eHarlequin.com

REQUEST YOUR FREE BOOKS!

2 FREE NOVELS PLUS 2 FREE GIFTS!

HARLEQUIN®

Blaze™

Red-hot reads!

YES! Please send me 2 FREE Harlequin® Blaze™ novels and my 2 FREE gifts (gifts are worth about $10). After receiving them, if I don't wish to receive any more books, I can return the shipping statement marked "cancel." If I don't cancel, I will receive 6 brand-new novels every month and be billed just $4.24 per book in the U.S. or $4.71 per book in Canada. That's a savings of 15% off the cover price. It's quite a bargain. Shipping and handling is just 50¢ per book.* I understand that accepting the 2 free books and gifts places me under no obligation to buy anything. I can always return a shipment and cancel at any time. Even if I never buy another book, the two free books and gifts are mine to keep forever.

151 HDN EYS2 351 HDN EYTE

Name	(PLEASE PRINT)	
Address		Apt. #
City	State/Prov.	Zip/Postal Code

Signature (if under 18, a parent or guardian must sign)

Mail to the Harlequin Reader Service:
IN U.S.A.: P.O. Box 1867, Buffalo, NY 14240-1867
IN CANADA: P.O. Box 609, Fort Erie, Ontario L2A 5X3

Not valid to current subscribers of Harlequin Blaze books.

Want to try two free books from another line?
Call 1-800-873-8635 or visit www.morefreebooks.com.

* Terms and prices subject to change without notice. Prices do not include applicable taxes. N.Y. residents add applicable sales tax. Canadian residents will be charged applicable provincial taxes and GST. Offer not valid in Quebec. This offer is limited to one order per household. All orders subject to approval. Credit or debit balances in a customer's account(s) may be offset by any other outstanding balance owed by or to the customer. Please allow 4 to 6 weeks for delivery. Offer available while quantities last.

Your Privacy: Harlequin Books is committed to protecting your privacy. Our Privacy Policy is available online at www.eHarlequin.com or upon request from the Reader Service. From time to time we make our lists of customers available to reputable third parties who may have a product or service of interest to you. If you would prefer we not share your name and address, please check here. ☐

HB09R3

HARLEQUIN *Blaze*

COMING NEXT MONTH
Available October 27, 2009

#501 MORE BLAZING BEDTIME STORIES Julie Leto and Leslie Kelly
Encounters
Fairy tales have never been so hot! Let bestselling authors Julie Leto and Leslie Kelly tell you a bedtime story that will inspire you to do anything but sleep!

#502 POWER PLAY Nancy Warren
Forbidden Fantasies
Forced to share a hotel room one night with a sexy hockey-playing cop, Emily Saunders must keep her hands to herself. Not easy for a massage therapist who's just *itching* to touch Jonah Betts's gorgeous muscles. But all bets are off when he suddenly makes a play for her!

#503 HOT SPELL Michelle Rowen
The Wrong Bed
As a modern-day ghost buster, Amanda LeGrange is used to dealing with the unexplained. But when an ancient spell causes her to fall into bed with her sexy enemy, she's definitely flustered. Especially since he's made it clear he likes her hands on him when they're out of bed, as well....

#504 HOLD ON TO THE NIGHTS Karen Foley
Dressed to Thrill
Hollywood's hottest heartthrob, Graeme Hamilton, is often called the world's sexiest bachelor. Only Lara Whitfield knows the truth. Sure, Graeme's sexy enough.... But he's very much married—to her!

#505 *SEALED* AND DELIVERED Jill Monroe
Uniformly Hot!
Great bod—check. Firm, kissable lips—check. Military man—check. Hailey Sutherland has found *the* guy to share some sexy moments with. In charge of SEAL training, Nate Peterson's not shocked by much, but he is by Hailey's attitude. He just hopes the gorgeous woman can handle as much attitude in the bedroom....

#506 ZERO CONTROL Lori Wilde
Though Roxanne Stanley put the *girl* in girl-next-door, she *wants* Dougal Lockhart. Now! What she doesn't know: the hottie security expert is undercover at the sensual fantasy resort to expose a criminal, but it may be her own secret that gets exposed....